The Crying Winds

THE CRYING WINDS

J.H. Rhodes

Text Copyright © 1980 by J.H. Rhodes

Published by 47North
P.O. Box 400818
Las Vegas, NV 89140

ISBN-13: 9781477837764
ISBN-10: 1477837760

The Crying Winds

CHAPTER ONE

Each revolution of the wheels on the huge bus brought Lori Hudson closer to her destination. A destination she had not sought out but had accepted with a kind of halfhearted resignation.

Looking through the window of the bus, Lori gazed without a great deal of interest at the dry New Mexico landscape. At first it had been a change from the rich greenery of Ohio, but now it had begun to take on a sameness that irritated her.

She knew that she would be unhappy at her Aunt Hannah's hotel. What was the name of it again? Lori searched through her purse until she found the dog-eared letter from her aunt, her father's spinster sister. Here it was—The House of the Crying Winds. The very name sent a chill through Lori's slim nineteen-year-old body.

Casually she brushed a strand of tawny hair away from her emerald green eyes. Not just green eyes, as her mother had often teased her, but the traditional Hudson emerald green.

Lori wondered what her parents were doing at this very moment. This had been the year Frank Hudson had retired from the pharmaceutical business he owned. He had made a vow to his wife, Sarah, that when he retired they would go to Europe for two glorious months. It would be the second honeymoon he had promised her years ago. Of course, nobody wanted a nineteen-year-old daughter around on a honeymoon.

So it had been Frank who had said, "And what are your plans for the summer, Lori?"

Lori, who would be a college sophomore in the fall, did not have to work her way through school, as some of her friends had to. Her father had set up a trust fund for that. So her social calendar was empty, waiting for any worthwhile suggestions.

"I haven't made any plans...yet," Lori had said.

"What about that young man of yours, Blaine Edwards?" her father had asked.

"That's between Lori and Blaine, dear," her mother had said tactfully.

Whatever had been between Lori and Blaine had ended with the school term. Blaine had made it quite clear that he didn't want to be tied down, that he was going to thumb his way around the country for the next year. If Lori wished to join him, she would be welcome. She had declined.

"Well, then, if you don't have any plans, why don't you help your Aunt Hannah this summer?" her dad had suggested. "She could use you at that hotel she owns in New Mexico."

"Aunt Hannah!" Lori had said incredulously. "I don't even know her! We've never met."

"There's one way to remedy that. Go to New Mexico and meet her."

"I don't know. New Mexico seems so far away."

Her father had smiled at her. "It might be good for you, Lori. Although it would be hard work. Maybe you couldn't handle it."

That did it as far as Lori was concerned. She knew that she had been pampered and spoiled to some extent all her life. Being an only child had its advantages. It also had a tendency to make one too dependent.

"Of course, I can handle it!" she said emphatically. "How do I get in touch with Aunt Hannah?"

Lori saw a proud gleam in her father's eye as he reached inside his shirt pocket. He handed her a letter.

"This came last week. I've been delaying answering it until I had something to write Hannah."

Lori quickly glanced at the bold, straightforward handwriting. The letter was brief, explaining how Hannah Hudson had bought a hotel but was finding it hard to keep help. She thought she could make a go of it if she could only find someone to assist her for the summer months.

"...Whoever it is must be reliable. The work isn't too hard, and I'll provide room and board and a salary...."

Lori had folded the letter and held it in her hand. "How can I turn down room and board and a salary?" she said with a shrug of her shoulders.

"Then you'll go?" her father asked.

"It might be interesting. I've never seen New Mexico. But what a strange name for a hotel. The House of the Crying Winds."

Her father leaned back with a relieved sigh. "I'll write your Aunt Hannah that you've accepted the job offer. As for the name, I'm sure my sister will be more than happy to fill you in on that. Hannah is quite a character. She's open, frank, and she's spent most of her life in the outdoors. She's a determined, independent person with a mind of her own. Eccentric—and smart enough to have become rich playing the stock market."

Two weeks after that talk with her dad and mother, Lori had boarded a jet and, after a changeover in Chicago, had arrived in Albuquerque in the early afternoon.

Here she caught a bus, which was the only way to get to Santa Inez. Aunt Hannah had told her that The House of the Crying Winds was about twenty miles from Santa

Inez. Someone would meet her when she arrived in the small town.

With a sigh, Lori leaned back in her seat. She wondered now if she had been hasty in her decision to help her aunt. If things didn't go well between Aunt Hannah and herself, she could always return to Ohio. But was that any solution to her overall problem?

Just what is my problem? Lori wondered. Have I grown too dependent on my parents? Have things been just too easy for me all my life? Lori realized that she must make a go of this summer in New Mexico. Not only for her parents' sake but for her own as well.

She tried to focus her attention on the passing scenery. The dun-colored land held a certain fascination, after all. And in the distance she saw flat-topped mesas framed against the farther mountains, which were shadowed in a smoky-blue haze. Surely she could endure New Mexico for a couple of months.

In the seat next to Lori, a woman who had also gotten on in Albuquerque stirred and awakened. Her name was Bessie and she had chatted nervously for a few miles, then closed her eyes and taken a nap.

"Where did you say you were headed for?" Bessie asked in her open, friendly way.

"My Aunt Hannah's. She just bought a hotel a few months ago, and I'm going to help out for the summer."

Bessie appeared pleased. "That's right kind of you. A pretty young thing like you giving up her summer to help run a hotel. You watch yourself now. Never can tell what kind of people might be staying there."

Lori fought to suppress a smile. She knew Bessie meant well. But after all, she was nineteen years old and fully capable of taking care of herself.

"What's the name of your aunt's place?"

"It's called The House of the Crying Winds. Have you ever heard of it?"

Bessie shook her head. "I live in Albuquerque. Just come to Santa Inez to visit my sister twice a year. Got to admit that's a peculiar name for a hotel. What's your aunt like?"

"We've never met. She's never left New Mexico that I know of. I've seen a few very old photographs of her. Still, I wouldn't know her if she stepped aboard the bus."

Bessie clicked her teeth. "Don't worry, dear. You'll get along just fine. Who wouldn't like a nice, unspoiled girl like yourself?"

At the mention of the word unspoiled, Lori inwardly cringed. She was not at all the person Bessie had supposed her to be. Then again Bessie didn't know her and she had tried to be herself. Maybe there was hope for her, after all.

Lori admired a silver ring that Bessie wore on her right index finger. It had a robin's egg blue stone.

"It's turquoise. My late husband gave it to me years ago. That was when turquoise was easy to come by. Turquoise is almost as valuable as gold now."

"It's beautiful," Lori said.

"Thanks, dear. Even though it's very valuable, I wouldn't part with it for anything. You know, sentiment and all that."

Lori nodded. Bessie was a squat, dumpy woman with a sweet face. She could tell that Bessie was still devoted to her late husband.

"In those days you could buy almost any Indian jewelry except pawn."

"What's pawn?" Lori asked.

"Well, you know, like when you pawn something. Indians did it, too. And turquoise is very precious to them.

If they got low in money, they would take a piece of turquoise to a trading post. The trader would appraise the turquoise and keep it in the store. Then the Indian would take what he needed in the way of supplies. The pawn turquoise was never sold. When the owner raised enough money, he would redeem the pawn turquoise."

As much as she tried not to become too interested in what Bessie was saying, Lori found herself fascinated by the woman's story. She also found herself glancing out the window with heightened interest.

Was she mistaken or was the sky the color of the ring Bessie wore on her finger? She had better watch herself or she might become attached to this land. And that would never do. After all, Lori only planned on spending the summer at her Aunt Hannah's.

Once she was started, it was hard to stop Bessie from spinning one tale after another. She seemed to know so much about the Indians and the history of the land.

Lori and Bessie talked until the bus came to an abrupt halt. Lori cast a sidelong glance out the window and saw they had arrived at Santa Inez.

When they had gotten off the bus, a woman with two shy children came rushing toward them. She turned out to be Bessie's sister.

After Bessie had introduced them, she said, "Lori's working this summer at a place called The House of the Crying Winds."

When she said these words, Lori couldn't help noticing a slight change in Bessie's sister's face.

"The House of the Crying Winds! Are you sure that's where you're going?"

"Why, yes," Lori answered, somewhat shaken by the woman's rather stern face. "Then you've heard of it. It's my Aunt Hannah's place."

"Hannah Hudson!" the woman said and the shadow left

her face. "Are you kin of Hannah's?"

"I'm her niece. She's my father's sister. Do you know her?"

The woman chuckled. "Everyone around these parts knows Hannah Hudson. She's quite a character. She's a little gruff sometimes, but that's just a put-on. Underneath all that bluster she's a softie."

Lori was relieved to hear those words. She decided she must have been mistaken when she thought she had seen a shadow of doubt come over the woman's face at the mention of the hotel.

"Did you say someone was supposed to meet you, dear?" Bessie asked as she looked around the almost deserted bus station.

"That's what Aunt Hannah wrote. Only, she didn't mention who it might be."

"We'll wait with you until whoever it is comes," Bessie said emphatically.

"That won't be necessary," Lori said. "I'm sure someone will come for me. They're probably just late in arriving. You run along. I know that you and your sister have a lot to talk over."

Bessie appeared uneasy. "Well, okay, if you're sure you'll be all right. Here's our phone number and our address. You call me when you get there so I won't be worried about you. Promise?"

Lori promised and after a quick good-bye Bessie and the others got into a battered station wagon and were gone.

When they had disappeared in a cloud of dust, Lori suddenly felt all alone. It had been like saying good-bye to an old friend. Watch it, kiddo, next thing you know you'll be telling a policeman you're lost, Lori chided herself. These unspoken words restored her sagging spirits.

Looking around, she saw a building housing a small office and waiting room. There was someone inside the office and she purposefully walked toward it.

Inside, she found a white-haired, wizened old man who was tagging some luggage.

"Pardon me," she said, "I was supposed to be met by someone from The House of the Crying Winds. Has anyone been asking for me? My name is Lori Hudson."

The old man looked up at her through bifocals that had slipped down the bridge of his nose.

"Hudson, you say? No, there hasn't been anyone here asking for you."

"Is there a phone I can use?"

The old man pushed his glasses up on his nose. "There is. Only, it won't do you any good to use it. Out of order. Won't be fixed until tomorrow."

Lori's disappointment must have shown on her face. The old man gestured with a sweep of his arm. "Might as well take a seat. If someone's coming to meet you, they'll no doubt come here first."

Sitting on a hard, unyielding bench, Lori kept her eyes on her luggage, which she could see through the dusty window. Had Aunt Hannah gotten confused or maybe even forgotten that she was to arrive today?

She suddenly realized how little she knew of her father's sister. The photographs she had been shown were old and somewhat out of focus. She knew from her father's description that Hannah Hudson was tall and thin with short-cropped, iron-gray hair. Beyond that, and the fact that she was strong-willed, Lori knew nothing about her. She would not have recognized the woman had she walked into the waiting room.

So far, Lori thought with a tinge of despair, her arrival at Santa Inez had not been particularly encouraging.Here she was, miles from home in an unfamiliar part of the country and all alone. Her earlier brave thoughts somehow had a hollow ring to them now that she was faced with the reality of the situation.

If there had been another bus at that moment headed in the direction of Albuquerque, she was almost certain she would be tempted to board it and leave Aunt Hannah to her problems. What if no one came to pick her up? She was almost ready to panic.

Lori was so wrapped up in her thoughts that she did not hear the door to the waiting room open. Nor did she hear footsteps until she felt the presence of someone standing over her. She glanced up into the unshaven face of a man who was wearing dirt-smeared Levi's and a denim shirt that clung to his muscular chest.

"You Lori Hudson?" he said as he stared down at her with his gold-flecked brown eyes that seemed to be mocking her from beneath bushy blond eyebrows.

Lori didn't like his manner and the way he was staring at her. "Yes, I am, if that's any concern of yours."

The blond giant grinned, showing white, even teeth. "No concern of mine. But your Aunt Hannah might be interested in you."

At the mention of her aunt's name, Lori sprang to her feet. "Thank goodness someone came. I was starting to feel very helpless, frightened. Were you sent by my aunt to meet me? Are you from the hotel?"

"Yes to both questions. It's getting late and I'm in a hurry. Where are your things?"

Lori definitely did not like his attitude. If he was an example of the help her aunt had hired, then it wasn't any wonder that the hotel was in trouble. She pointed to the place where her luggage stood and was forced to follow him outside. Whoever he was, he made her feel like a little child following obediently in his footsteps.

The blond giant tossed her luggage into the back of a

pickup that was as dust-smeared as he was. He didn't even bother opening the door for her. Lori slid onto the seat next to him, keeping as much distance as she could between the two of them.

"You said you were from the hotel?" she remarked inanely.

As he started the pickup, he said, "Uh-huh. Name's Rex Fraser. You'll be seeing a lot of me."

Not if I can help it, Lori said to herself.

CHAPTER TWO

Rex Fraser seemed to drive the pickup as though he took delight in hitting every chuckhole in the road. Lori was determined that she would not complain, for she felt that would be just the reaction the surly blond giant would be expecting. She hooked her knees under the dashboard to ease the impact of the jostling.

After hitting an unusually deep rut in the road, Rex turned to her and said, "That's the last of the rough stretch. You can relax now."

"Thanks," Lori said, not bothering to hide the venom in her voice. "Have you been here long?"

"You mean at the Crying Winds? Not very. It suits my purposes. What do you think of New Mexico?"

"So far it's hardly the land of enchantment."

Rex laughed. It was a deep, low-pitched sound. Rugged, like the man he was. "If you don't like it, you can always go back home. Wherever that is."

"Ohio. And I have no desire to return there until the end of the summer. I made a promise to my aunt that I'd help her. That's what I intend doing."

"A good speech. Who wrote it for you?"

Lori sputtered and fumed. How dare this man say such things to her! He hardly knew her.

"I meant every word I said. You may not believe this,

Mr. Fraser, but when I make up my mind, nothing or nobody can change it."

Rex snorted. "You haven't been to Crying Winds yet. It's just possible you might have to eat those words."

"You're impossible!" Lori snapped and turned her attention to the passing scenery.

The sun had begun to touch the upper peaks of the faraway mountains, and there was a sudden coolness in the air. The sky had changed from its turquoise color to a dark amethyst. Shadows were beginning to fall across the pinon trees and the gray-colored plants. This part of New Mexico appeared to Lori to be lonely and desolate.

Suddenly, Rex Fraser's words sank into her mind. "What did you mean by that last remark?" she asked. "And why do you call it Crying Winds?"

"To answer your last question, it's quite a mouthful to say The House of the Crying Winds all the time. So I shortened it. As to the first question, Crying Winds is pretty isolated. The only thing for miles around is an Indian pueblo and that was vacated years ago."

"What's a pueblo? I mean, I've heard the word. But I don't know exactly what it is."

"You are a tenderfoot, aren't you?"

Lori pretended to ignore his remark.

"Pueblos are villages built by the Indians years ago," Rex Fraser said. "You'll find them scattered all over the state. This particular pueblo has a legend attached to it. Seems the Indians abandoned it in a hurry for some unknown reason. But they supposedly left a fortune in turquoise behind. People have combed the ruins for years, but so far they haven't found the turquoise."

"Do you believe there's turquoise buried there?"

Rex shrugged. "It makes a good legend. A newcomer like you would swallow that tale hook, line, and sinker."

For a moment Lori had actually found herself drawn

to the surly blond man. Rex Fraser, despite his shabby appearance, had a certain charm. But that had only been for a moment. His true self was constantly revealed by the snide tone of his comments.

Well, she wouldn't fall into that trap again. When she got to Crying Winds, she would have a little talk with her aunt. She was certain that her Aunt Hannah wouldn't condone his attitude toward her.

Then Lori wondered if perhaps her aunt was used to Rex Fraser. Maybe this was the way guests were treated at Crying Winds. After all, rugged New Mexico was a far cry from civilized Ohio.

The road began to wind up a slight rise. And when they had reached its summit, Rex Fraser suddenly braked the pickup.

"What's wrong?" Lori asked with alarm.

"Nothing. I just thought you'd like to get your first view of Crying Winds from here. It's down there."

Lori looked in the direction Rex was pointing. Below, she could see a long, sprawling adobe house. Even in the dim light the house appeared to shimmer with a dun-colored glow. Lori's heart sank. There was nothing for miles around but the hotel. It was the most desolate place she could imagine.

"Want to turn around and go back to Santa Inez?" she heard Rex Fraser say in a taunting tone of voice.

"I came this far, I might as well go all the way. But why my aunt would buy such an out-of-the-way place I'll never know."

"She does all right. There are guests at the place, believe it or not. For some reason travelers hear about Crying Winds. As a matter of fact, there's a movie star living there right now."

Lori couldn't help staring at Rex incredulously. "A movie star? There? What's his name?"

"It's a she. Her name's Isabel Jessop."

Lori turned the name over in her mind. She had never heard of Isabel Jessop before. "The name doesn't mean a thing to me."

"Don't let Isabel Jessop hear you say that. To hear her tell it, she was the reigning queen of the screen. Only, she never tells when she sat on the throne. I think she's a phony."

Phony or not, Lori was suddenly anxious to meet the woman. Anyway, she doubted that a man like Rex Fraser would know a movie star if one came up and bit him. As she thought that, a smile crossed her full lips and she felt her old confidence returning.

"You look like the cat that just had a juicy, fat canary for lunch," he said.

"Something like that," Lori answered. "Well, are we going to sit here all day, or do you intend driving on?"

"Your wish is my command."

"Then I command you to get moving," Lori replied.

Her sarcasm was wasted on Rex Fraser. He merely shrugged as he continued the drive to Crying Winds. There was a smug, self-satisfied smile on his lips that bothered Lori. It was as though he held a secret, a secret he had no intention of sharing with her.

The road widened once they were down from the slight rise and it was in much better condition. Lori noticed, with some annoyance, now that the road was smooth and passable, Rex drove slower. He was obviously doing everything he could to make this ride as unenjoyable for her as possible.

As they drew closer to the hotel, Lori got a better look at the long, one-storied structure made of adobe. The entire hotel was built around a patio in the shape of a rectangle. There was a wrought-iron gate which stretched along the front portion of the house. Not far from the house was a rather ornately printed sign announcing THE HOUSE OF THE CRYING WINDS.

Rex once again braked the pickup. "Welcome to the Crying Winds."

Lori did not hesitate in opening the door and getting out of the truck. As she did so, she was met by a sudden blast of cool wind. She shivered in her cotton dress as Rex slammed the door to the pickup.

The wind moving through the pinon trees made a mournful, crying sound. She suspected how the hotel had come by its name.

While Rex was busy getting her luggage from the bed of the truck, Lori moved toward the wrought-iron gate. From the other side, she saw the movement of someone as the person walked purposefully toward the gate. At first Lori thought, from the attire and the walk, it was a man. Then, as the gate swung inward, she saw it was a woman. A woman with iron-gray hair cut short and combed back over her ears.

"Lori? Is that you?" asked the harsh, stern voice of the woman.

It had to be her Aunt Hannah.

"Aunt Hannah?" Lori said uncertainly as she walked toward the woman.

Aunt Hannah extended a hand and Lori took it in hers. The hand was smooth to the touch, not calloused as Lori had imagined it would be from the looks of her aunt. Hannah Hudson wore denims and a cotton shirt. Her feet were clad in scuffed boots.

"I was beginning to get worried about you. Did you have a good trip?"

"It was smooth sailing from Ohio to Albuquerque. The bus to Santa Inez was a little late, but I met a very nice woman and we had a good chat."

"Let me look at you. Yep, you're Frank's daughter, all

right. Only, you could use a few pounds. Look kinda puny."

Her father had been right. Aunt Hannah was outspoken and direct.

"I'm stronger than I look," Lori said. "I'm looking forward to helping you this summer."

Quick frown lines formed on Aunt Hannah's forehead. "We'll talk about that later. You must be hungry. I'll show you to your room, and you can freshen up. Got to get some meat on those bones."

By this time Rex Fraser had unloaded the pickup.

"Much obliged to you for picking up my niece, Mr. Fraser," Aunt Hannah said.

"No trouble at all. Glad to help out," Rex said with a smile.

Lori thought her aunt was being far too formal with the hired help. Wait until she learned how Rex had treated her on the ride from Santa Inez! If her aunt had to be so polite, there was no reason she had to follow suit.

"Bring my luggage to my room," Lori told Rex over her shoulder, and she couldn't help noticing the surprised look on her aunt's face. "Come, Aunt Hannah, you did say you'd show me my room. I'm dying to see the inside of the hotel."

Lori was tempted to put an arm around her aunt's waist, but Hannah Hudson was far too stiff and unbending for such a gesture. In a way Lori was being lighthearted to make up for her uneasiness. She had been forewarned that Aunt Hannah was a character, but she hadn't expected her to be so aloof.

But then, what could she expect? This was the first time the two of them had met. Lori told herself that she shouldn't jump to any hasty conclusions as far as her aunt was concerned.

Aunt Hannah led her through the patio, which had a concrete floor. Scattered around the patio were huge brown vases filled with cacti.

"You don't have to fret over them," her aunt said. "A little water goes a long way with those things."

They left the patio and entered the first door on the left, which led to a combination office and living room. The floor was a glistening red tile. Indian throw rugs in muted colors were scattered about the long, spacious room. The furniture was all leather and very sturdy and functional, including the registration desk.

Next to an oval fireplace was a shelf holding an array of small dolls.

"How interesting. What kind of dolls are they?" Lori asked.

"Kachinas. The Indians make them and give them to the children during certain celebrations. Dust catchers every last one of them."

Lori was somewhat dismayed at her aunt's attitude. If that was how she felt about the dolls, Lori wondered why Hannah had ever gone to the trouble of collecting them.

Before she could speak, a second door to the room was flung open and a woman made a dramatic entrance. Her hair was the color of a discarded orange peel. The makeup on her face must have been layers deep. Yet there was a certain attractiveness to the woman's face that commanded attention.

"Miss Hudson, has there been a letter for me?" she asked Aunt Hannah. "I am expecting an important letter from my agent."

Aunt Hannah gave an exasperated sigh. "I told you, Miss Jessop, the mail comes at noon. If there had been anything for you, I'd have let you know."

The woman sniffed. "Very well. But do let me know

the moment any mail arrives for me."

The woman saw Lori for the first time. "Are you a new guest?"

'This is my niece, Lori," Aunt Hannah said. "She's here to help out for the summer. Lori, this is Isabel Jessop."

"Charmed," Isabel said and Lori could see how the woman could be that very word. She was every inch the actress.

"Very pleased to meet you. I'm told that you're connected with the motion-picture business," Lori said.

Isabel Jessop lit up like a Christmas tree. "I was a star of the first magnitude."

"I'm sure you were very good."

Isabel turned to Hannah Hudson. "You have a jewel here, Miss Hudson. We'll get along just fine." She smiled at Lori. "Someday, dear, remind me to show you my scrapbook of clippings."

With that Isabel Jessop made a grand exit.

"Wow! What a performance," Lori said after the woman had gone.

"And that was just what it was. A performance," Aunt Hannah said. "You never can tell with that woman whether she's telling the truth or just acting."

Lori could tell that Aunt Hannah had not been impressed by Isabel Jessop.

"How many rooms do you have here, Aunt Hannah?"

"Ten. That doesn't include your room and mine. We stay here. That is, our rooms are separate from the guest section."

Lori was beginning to warm up to her aunt, although she wasn't certain that Aunt Hannah had fully accepted her as a niece yet.

"I'm dying to know more about the hotel. And how did

you ever come up with a name like The House of the Crying Winds? It's so unusual."

By this time Aunt Hannah had taken a seat on an easy chair. Lori sat down on one of the leather couches. Above her hung a wrought-iron chandelier. Lori tried not to notice the cobwebs that had formed around the light fixture. Nor did she focus her attention too long on the dust that was layered throughout the room. It was obvious that Aunt Hannah did need some help as far as cleaning was concerned.

"I've had the place about ten months now. A friend of mine told me about it. Seems it was built by a millionaire from California. He had it built for his wife. But she died shortly after it was completed. He never wanted to see it after that. So I got it fairly cheap.

"Out here you'll find at night that the winds hit the place because it's not too well protected. When I heard the noise the wind made through the pinons, it had a wailing sound to it. So I called the place The House of the Crying Winds."

Lori had been listening intently. She was glad she had been right in her earlier guess about the origin of the hotel's name. When her aunt finished, she asked, "How many guests are staying here at the present time?"

"Let's see now. You've met Isabel Jessop. And there's a man in number 5 named Oscar T. Owens. A real character. I think he's a salesman of some sort. Then there's an older couple, Ray and Nancy Neeley, in number 8. And, of course, you've met the man in number 10. Rex Fraser."

Lori gasped, "Rex Fraser! You mean he's a guest at the hotel?"

Aunt Hannah nodded. "I thought you knew. Didn't he tell you? He volunteered to pick you up at Santa Inez, since I couldn't leave the hotel at the time."

Lori's cheeks flamed. How could she face the man after the way she had acted toward him? She didn't have much choice in the matter, for at that moment the door opened and Rex Fraser entered with her luggage.

CHAPTER THREE

"Where do you want these put?" Rex Fraser asked with a mocking look in his gold-flecked eyes.

"Just set them down, Mr. Fraser," Aunt Hannah said with a sidelong glance at Lori. "If you two will excuse me, I have to see Mr. Owens. He was complaining about something earlier today."

After Aunt Hannah had gone, Lori said, "What must you think of me? I'm sorry for speaking to you so harshly. And you being a paying guest and all."

Rex laughed. "In a way it was my fault. I should have told you who I was. But I never got around to it. At least I know you're capable of handling the help. If there were any at Crying Winds."

"Would you like to sit down for a moment?" Lori said, the redness finally leaving her cheeks.

Rex took a seat across from her.

"How did you happen to come to Crying Winds, Mr. Fraser?" she asked quietly.

"Why don't you call me Rex? I'd like that better. Mr. Fraser sounds too formal for my liking."

"Only if you call me Lori."

"It's a deal. You asked me how I happened to be staying here. I'm a freelance photographer. I make my living selling pictures. At the moment I'm doing a series on the

Southwest. Crying Winds is a stopover while I get some good shots of the country. Particularly the pueblo."

"A photographer! That sounds exciting. Does it pay well?"

Rex smiled. Underneath his dust-spattered face, she could tell that there was a handsome man. "Pretty good. But more than that, I'm my own boss. I can go wherever I choose and stay as long as it suits me."

"That sounds like a very interesting life. But how does your wife feel about you being gone all the time?"

"If I had a wife, she'd have to be the type who enjoyed traveling."

Rex Fraser had plainly stated his marital status. Lori wondered why she was relieved to find that he was not married. After all, only a short while ago she had found Rex Fraser to be a very disagreeable person. Had he changed that quickly, or had she been the one who had changed?

"Do you think you're going to like being in such an isolated place?" Rex said.

"I don't know. All I can do is try to do my best to like it here."

"Anybody special you'll miss back in Ohio?"

Lori knew what Rex was getting at. "There was my mother and father, but by this time they're in Europe on vacation. As far as a boyfriend is concerned, that ended when the school term was finished."

It did not take a genius to see the change in Rex Fraser's attitude when she told him she was unattached at the moment.

"When you get some time off, I'd like to show you around, if you're interested," Rex said.

"That sounds like fun. Only, I have to see what my aunt's plans are for me. After all, I am a working girl."

"At least I'll be seeing you at breakfast, lunch, and dinner."

"So you will. Where are the meals served, by the way?"

"Meals are served in the dining room. The dining room is through that door over there. The kitchen connects with it."

Lori gazed in the direction Rex had pointed. "At least I'll be able to help Aunt Hannah out with the food. If I do say so myself, I am a fairly good cook. My mother saw to that. So I wouldn't starve to death in college."

Rex grinned. "I'm beginning to think you have a good chance of surviving, Lori Hudson. Maybe you're not as helpless and scared as I thought you were."

The words rankled Lori. "You shouldn't judge someone by first impressions, Mr. Fraser."

Rex held up his hands. "Truce. If that sounded like male chauvinism, I apologize. That's the last thing I wanted to do. Make you angry and make you call me by my last name."

Lori couldn't help smiling at Rex. He was sincere and he did have a certain charm that appealed to her. "Truce."

The door opened and Aunt Hannah appeared, followed by a man with a flushed face. The man's hair was beginning to thin and his gray eyes appeared to be too close to his large nose. He was wearing a loud, orange-colored shirt with a string tie that appeared to be sinking into the roll of flesh at his neck.

"Oscar T. Owens is the name," he said. "You must be Miss Hudson's niece. Just what this old place needs, a pretty, young face."

Before Lori could say anything, the beefy man took one of her hands in his. She winced at the surprising strength in his fingers.

"Yes, indeed. I've been all over this vast nation," he

went on. "Just name a state, I've been there. In my line of work I travel a lot."

"Just exactly what is your line of work, Mr. Owens?" Lori asked.

"Sales. I'm in sales. Anything and all things."

With that Oscar T. Owens launched into a long story of his life as a salesman. As much as Lori tried not to be amused by the outgoing man, she found herself laughing at his funny stories. But she felt that a little of Oscar T. Owens went a long way.

While Oscar was talking, she happened to glance at Rex, who shook his head in amusement. Aunt Hannah also appeared to enjoy the rapid flow of conversation.

Finally Oscar T. Owens came to an abrupt end. "But that's enough for now. After all, Lori, you're going to be here for the summer. You'll have plenty of time to listen to my adventures. See you all at dinner."

Saying those words, Oscar walked out of the room. The silence after he had gone was almost deafening.

"I'd better run along, too," Rex said, getting to his feet.

"Thanks again for driving me in from Santa Inez," Lori said.

"My pleasure. Take care," Rex said.

When he had gone, Aunt Hannah said, "Come along, Lori. I'll show you your room. You'll want to get settled in, I'm sure."

Lori followed her aunt into a room that branched off from the living room. It was small but cozy. There were Indian blankets scattered about on the floor, and on the chest of drawers were two kachina dolls. Sliding glass doors opened onto the patio. There was also a window facing the patio. In the distance, Lori could see the first clear stars of evening beginning to twinkle in a darkened sky.

"This is wonderful, Aunt Hannah," Lori said. "I know I'm going to love being here."

"Are you sure?" Aunt Hannah said. "After all, you're in a pretty isolated place. There isn't much here for a young girl like yourself. And maybe the work will be too much for you."

Lori could tell that her aunt was giving her the option of leaving. She knew that Crying Winds was a long way from anywhere. Perhaps after the novelty wore off, she would regret not having returned to Ohio. But she was determined to stay, to prove her independence, her strength of character.

"You can't get rid of me that easily, Aunt Hannah. You're a Hudson, so you must know that we're a stubborn bunch. I plan on staying for the entire summer. And I plan on helping you as much as I can."

Aunt Hannah shrugged. It was difficult for Lori to tell whether her aunt was pleased with her decision or not. Hannah Hudson was such a stoic person.

"Well, I gave you a chance, Lori. If you want to help, I can use you in the kitchen after you get settled."

Aunt Hannah opened the door to the small hallway which led to the living room. "Don't pay too much attention to the way I act, Lori. I've been on my own all my life. Guess maybe I'm a stern old thing. You're welcome to stay here."

Lori continued to stare at the closed door for a few seconds after her aunt had gone. In her odd way Aunt Hannah had welcomed her to Crying Winds.

She wondered if she would ever get used to the woman's gruff behavior. Even though she had been warned by her father that Aunt Hannah was a peculiar person, she hadn't expected her to be so cold and unapproachable.

Then, with a shrug, Lori turned to face her room. She

realized she didn't have her luggage with her. So she went to get it from the living room.

Back in her room again, she opened her luggage and hung up some dresses, skirts, jeans, and blouses in a small closet near the chest of drawers. Lori wondered if she had time for a quick shower, decided she did, stopped her unpacking, and stepped into the bathroom.

The pelting cold water refreshed her and raised chilly gooseflesh on her body. After she had dried herself on a fluffy towel, she slipped into a pair of wool pants and a soft coral sweater. Seating herself on a narrow bench before the oval mirror on her dressing table, she began to brush her tawny-colored hair.

Lori was thinking about her home and her mother and father, so when the face appeared at the window, she did not really pay any attention to it at first. Then her eyes became riveted to the ugly, scowling face that leered at her from the patio window.

It was the most horrible face she had ever seen, with eyes that stared at her with deep hatred and a mane of long black hair. The mouth was twisted in a hideous grimace.

Lori screamed and closed her eyes.

When she opened them again, the face was gone. There was a pounding at the door, and then it was flung open. Aunt Hannah marched into the room.

"What's going on here? Why did you let out that awful scream? It scared ten years off my life."

"I saw a face. A horrible face at the patio window."

Aunt Hannah strode across the room and looked out the window, then flung open the patio doors. Lori was right behind her. There was nobody on the patio. The only sound was the crying of the wind.

"Don't see anybody," Aunt Hannah said. "Are you sure you saw a face? Maybe you just imagined it."

At that moment Rex Fraser came into the room, followed by a wheezing Oscar T. Owens.

"Are you all right, Lori?" Rex said, and Lori found herself rushing instinctively into his protective arms.

"What in the world's going on here?" Oscar T. Owens said, mopping at his face with a checkered handkerchief. "I could hear that scream all the way over in my room."

"Lori's got the bugaboos. Claims she saw somebody looking in the window at her," her aunt said.

Lori recovered herself and eased herself out of Rex's arms.

"I didn't *think* I saw someone, I did see someone. It was a hideous face with a twisted mouth and hard, cold eyes. I've never seen anything like it in my life."

Aunt Hannah raised a skeptical eyebrow. "If you ask me, you're just overwrought from your trip. Appears your eyes are playing tricks on you."

"Did you search the patio?" Rex asked.

"Aunt Hannah and I both looked out there," Lori said. "Whoever it was is gone."

"If you don't mind, I'll have a look around," Rex said as he walked out to the patio.

"Your aunt's probably right, young lady. Who would be snooping around here looking in windows? Out in the middle of nowhere?" Oscar T. Owens said. "Besides, the way you described whoever it was doesn't sound human to me."

Lori's fright had passed. Now she was becoming angry. It was apparent that neither her aunt nor Oscar believed her story.

"You're acting like a silly, emotional schoolgirl," Oscar said.

"It doesn't matter whether you believe me or not. I know what I saw. And I'm not a silly, emotional schoolgirl."

At that moment Rex reappeared at the glass doors leading to the patio. He was holding something in his hands.

"Is this what you saw, Lori?" he asked as he turned the object over and held it upright.

It was a mask made from some kind of metal. Lori gave a loud gasp. It was the same face she had seen staring at her through the window and in the mirror.

"That's the face I saw," Lori said. "It's a mask!"

"I found it hidden in some mesquite outside. Whoever wore it was in a hurry to get rid of it."

Aunt Hannah looked at the mask carefully and then turned to Lori. "Guess you really did see something, after all. For a minute there, I thought it was just your imagination."

"What is that thing?" Oscar T. Owens asked in his loud, booming voice.

Rex turned the mask over in his hands. "I would say it was some sort of ceremonial mask that the Indians wear. What do you think, Hannah?"

Aunt Hannah's face was as much of a mask as the one Rex held in his hands. "Dare say you're right, Rex. I've seen a few in my time."

At that moment a man and a woman appeared at the door to Lori's room. They were both in their mid-sixties. The man was tall and thin with sharp features. The woman could almost have been his twin.

She was almost as tall as the man and even thinner. Standing in the doorway, they looked like two predatory birds waiting for a chance to pounce on an unwary victim.

"We heard a scream," said the man. "Would you mind telling us what's going on over here?"

Aunt Hannah walked over to the gaunt couple. "It was nothing. Just somebody playing a practical joke on my niece. Lori, I'd like you to meet Ray and Nancy Neeley. They're in number 8."

Lori managed a feeble greeting while the Neeleys merely looked at her.

"Lori will be helping me out this summer," Aunt Hannah said. "Help is so hard to come by these days."

"Doesn't look as though she's getting off to a very good start," Nancy Neeley said in a crisp tone of voice. "Come, Ray, we have to change for dinner."

As silently as they had appeared, the Neeleys were gone. Lori had held back from saying anything. After all, they were paying guests. But even so, there was something sinister about the Neeleys. She knew that she would never grow to like them.

"Now that the mystery is solved about the intruder, I have to get to the kitchen," Lori's aunt said.

"What about the mask?" Rex asked.

"Do what you wish with it," Aunt Hannah told him. "It was just somebody's idea of a joke."

Oscar T. Owens followed Aunt Hannah out of the room, chattering away. When they had gone, Lori turned to face Rex.

"You don't believe that it was a practical joke, do you?"

"Hardly. Someone's gone to a lot of trouble to frighten you."

"But why? I hardly know anyone here at the Crying Winds. It doesn't make sense. Unless whoever it was got the wrong room."

Rex frowned. "That might be. It would certainly appear that someone isn't very welcome at the Crying Winds."

"Have there been any other goings-on like this?"

Rex shook his head. "No. Things have been pretty quiet around here. Of course, I've only been here a few weeks. But it would appear that someone isn't too happy about your coming to the Crying Winds."

CHAPTER FOUR

After Rex had gone, Lori lingered in her room for a few minutes, turning over in her mind what had happened since she had arrived at The House of the Crying Winds. She had met her aunt, who appeared to be quite indifferent to her coming, not at all like her letter, which had hinted pleadingly that her niece help her.

Aunt Hannah was an extremely difficult person to get to know. Lori couldn't help feeling that perhaps her aunt was in some way disappointed in her. Well, I'll change her mind on that, Lori thought determinedly.

Then there were the guests at Crying Winds. Oscar T. Owens was a loud, blustery person whom she would try to avoid as much as possible. Isabel Jessop was interesting in a peculiar sort of way. It was possible that she had been in the movies, she was dramatic enough. Yet Lori felt it strange that she had never heard of the woman.

Without a doubt the Neeleys were a strange couple. They did not seem especially pleased to meet her. In fact, they had been downright rude.

The only person she felt at ease with was Rex Fraser. But when she had first met him, she had not felt that way at all.

Give them all a chance, Lori said to herself. You just

arrived here. Weren't you the one who told Rex not to judge a person by first impressions?

Lori felt better as she left the room and went across the hall to the living room.

Aunt Hannah was just hanging up the phone as she entered. The lights in the room played a brief trick on Lori's eyes. Aunt Hannah for a moment appeared to be younger than she was. Then she saw Lori and the illusion created by the lights vanished.

"Are you over your heebie-jeebies?" Aunt Hannah asked.

"Completely. Sorry about all the trouble I caused. Can I help?"

"If you set the table, that would be a big help," Aunt Hannah said in a not unfriendly tone of voice.

Lori followed her aunt into the dining room, which was also quite spacious and had a huge mahogany table in the center under another wrought-iron chandelier.

Aunt Hannah showed Lori where the dishes and glassware were. Then she hurried away to the kitchen, which was at the far end of the room.

As Lori set the table, she occasionally glanced out the windows, which offered an interesting view of the faraway mountains that were black juttings against the night sky.

When she had finished, her aunt walked in from the kitchen. "Looks real nice, Lori. You just might do, after all."

Lori felt that she had redeemed herself in her aunt's eyes after the awful episode with the mask earlier in the evening.

Aunt Hannah was carrying a platter of fried chicken, and Lori scurried into the kitchen, where she found a tray loaded with a crisp green salad and a large bowl of succotash.

When Lori came back into the dining room carrying the tray, Rex Fraser had arrived.

"That's looks delicious," Rex said as she arranged the food on the table. "Looks as though you've already started to work."

Lori grinned at him. "Don't you think it's about time I started earning my keep?"

Within a few minutes, the other guests had arrived and taken seats around the huge table. To Lori's surprise, both she and her aunt were to eat with the guests. Aunt Hannah placed Lori next to Rex, and she herself took a seat next to the garrulous Mr. Owens. Only, with Isabel Jessop in the room, Oscar was finding it difficult to be the center of attention.

"Crying Winds would make a marvelous setting for a movie," Isabel was saying. "Can't you just imagine a spine-tingling mystery going on here!"

It was Rex who spoke next. "There already seems to be one. Lori had an unpleasant experience in her room earlier."

"Really!" Isabel's watery blue eyes focused on Lori. "Tell me all about it. I simply adore mysteries."

Lori glanced briefly at her aunt, who did not appear in the least interested in what was going on around her.

As quickly as she could, Lori told the aging actress all about the frightening face and Rex's finding the ceremonial mask.

"How enthralling," Isabel said, not really liking to have someone else in the limelight. "Why on earth do you suppose anyone would want to frighten you?"

"Sounds to me as though it was somebody's idea of a practical joke," Ray Neeley said as he sipped a glass of water.

"I agree," his wife said, dismissing the entire matter.

"We came to Crying Winds expecting to find peace and quiet. And it has been. Up until now, at least."

Lori was about to apologize, but she saw a look in Rex's eyes which told her that she had no reason to.

"How long have you been at the hotel, Mrs. Neeley?" Lori said instead.

"About two weeks. My husband is retired. We travel a great deal. When we find a place we like, we stay on. Since we have no children, we have only ourselves to please."

Mentally Lori thought that summed up the Neeleys quite well.

"Do go on with your story, Lori," Isabel said. "This matter of the mask has aroused my curiosity."

"There isn't any more to tell. Rex has the mask now. And I'll be happy never to see it again."

"You must let me see it, Mr. Fraser," Isabel said. "Anything that hints of a mystery simply fascinates me. And have you been taking any interesting photographs lately?"

Rex nodded. "Quite a few. New Mexico has exceptional scenery. I particularly want to get some shots of the deserted pueblo."

"The pueblo?" Aunt Hannah said with a snort. "That's nothing but an old ruin. Can't for the life of me imagine anyone wanting to take pictures of that place."

"I agree with Miss Hudson," Oscar T. Owens said. "Sounds to me, Rex, as though you're just wasting film with that old dump."

Rex wasn't discouraged by what they were saying. "That's the whole purpose of my being here. I want to capture the old as well as the new for my series on the Southwest."

"That's a great idea, Rex," Lori said and got a disapproving glare from Aunt Hannah. "I would love to see the pueblo."

"You would!" Rex said with enthusiasm. "Great, we'll go there one of these evenings after work."

"How gallant," Isabel Jessop said with just a trace of sarcasm in her voice.

"That invitation includes you, Miss Jessop," Rex offered.

But Isabel shook her orange-tinted tresses. "Isabel, please. I'm afraid a jaunt in the wilds is not my thing. Although it was sweet of you to offer."

Lori was happy, in a way, that Isabel had declined the invitation. She wanted the trip to include only herself and Rex. Was that some of her old childishness coming back? She reminded herself that she had come here to acquire some independence, to shed her selfish old ways.

After dessert and coffee had been consumed, Lori told her aunt to join the others by the living-room fireplace while she did the dishes.

Aunt Hannah accepted graciously. Rex helped Lori pile up the dishes, but she drew the line at letting him help her wash them.

"It's what I'm being paid to do, Rex. I have to learn to accept responsibilities. Do you understand?"

"Yes. Good for you. When you finish, why don't you join us by the fireplace? I'm looking forward to that."

After Rex had gone and the dishes were soaking, Lori remembered that she had promised Bessie she would call. She found the woman's telephone number in her purse, which was in her room. Then she returned to the kitchen to make the call on the extension.

Bessie's sister answered and called Bessie to the phone. Hearing the woman's voice was like talking to an old friend, although Lori hardly knew her bus companion.

Bessie was relieved to learn Lori had made it to the hotel without any mishaps.

"You take care now, Lori. And don't work too hard. Come see us when you get a chance. You have my sister's address. I worry about you being out there in that wilderness."

"Nothing can happen to me here," Lori said, not daring to mention the episode of the mask to Bessie.

"Have you met any of the guests?" Bessie asked.

Lori told her all about the people who were staying at Crying Winds. When she mentioned Rex, Bessie said, "He sounds nice. Is he married?"

"No."

"A photographer, you say. Well, he sounds like he may be all right."

After that Lori and Bessie talked for a brief time, and then Lori hung up. Bessie was certainly an inquisitive, forceful person. But she meant well.

When the last dish had been washed, Lori went into the living room to join the others. Rex had saved a seat for her on the couch next to him. The crackling flames from the fireplace gave the long, spacious room a cheerful feeling.

"Fix yourself a brandy, Rex," Aunt Hannah said. "And pour one for Lori."

Lori almost never drank. But since Aunt Hannah had suggested she have a glass of brandy, she did not feel that she should refuse.

Isabel Jessop was reminiscing about her career in the movies. Lori noticed that the fading beauty very cleverly omitted mentioning the names of the movies she had appeared in.

Once, when Oscar T. Owens asked what movie she was describing, Isabel said, "My memory fades. Now wouldn't you know I just can't remember."

With that Isabel went on to discuss the movie, just explaining so much of the plot that the film might have been one of a dozen with a similar story line.

As Isabel paused dramatically for a sip of her brandy, the Neeleys seized the opportunity to arise simultaneously.

"If you will excuse us. It's getting late and my wife and I have had a long day," Ray Neeley said as they walked out of the living room.

Now that the Neeleys had gone, there was less tension in the room. There was something about the couple that disturbed Lori. It was as if they had a secret which they did not intend to share with anyone else.

"Anyone for a refill?" Oscar T. Owens said with one hand on the brandy bottle.

Everyone declined. Aunt Hannah did not try to disguise her obvious displeasure at Oscar for having another drink. He was already slurring his words, and his usually florid face was now a bright, glowing red.

Rex excused himself and went to his room. Then he brought back some pictures he had recently taken.

"These are excellent, Rex," Lori said. "You have a good eye for your subjects."

Isabel was more effusive in her praise, but she had an ulterior motive. The photographs helped her launch a story about some cameramen she had worked with in Hollywood.

Even though Isabel was interesting, Lori suddenly found her head nodding. She was fighting sleep.

"It would appear that I'm losing my audience," the actress said, and Lori shook her head to stay awake.

"I'm sorry. I guess all the excitement I've had today is beginning to catch up."

Isabel and a rather reluctant Oscar T. Owens got to their feet and, saying good night all around, departed.

Aunt Hannah yawned and said, "Tomorrow comes early. I'm going to bed. Wouldn't be a bad idea if you did the same, Lori."

After Aunt Hannah had said good night, Rex gathered up his photographs and put them inside a manila folder.

"Sorry I kept you up so late, Lori. I guess my enthusiasm got the better of me."

"Don't apologize. I enjoyed them. You have a real talent. It's just that for a moment there I got very sleepy."

"Well, I'll see you tomorrow. If you have any trouble, I'm in number 10. All you have to do is call me."

"I'll remember that. But I hope it was all just a practical joke, after all."

Rex left then. As Lori turned out the lights in the living room and went to her own room, she could not keep from thinking what a nice man Rex Fraser was.

Lori filled the tub with warm water and took a long, leisurely bath. Then she slipped on her pajamas and a robe before she went back into her room. The bath had relaxed her, but she found now she wasn't as sleepy as before.

She busied herself with more unpacking. The room was small but cozy. Occasionally, she glanced at the patio doors and the experience of a few hours earlier came rushing back to her.

Who had worn the mask? And why was that person trying to frighten her? Even if it was just a practical joke, it had been a cruel one. If she ever found out whom the mask belonged to, she would certainly give that person a good tongue-lashing. Knowing that Rex was only a few doors away made her feel better.

Lori wandered to the glass doors and gazed out at the sky full of bright, twinkling stars. The moon was full and its light bathed the patio in a bright, spectral glow. Out here in the open country the stars appeared nearer than back in Ohio. She felt that if she were outside, she could almost reach out and touch them.

Sliding the glass doors open, Lori slipped out to the patio. The moaning of the wind through the trees was quite loud. It sent a shiver down her spine. She gathered the robe closer to her throat with one hand.

Now that she was outside, Lori strolled to the adobe wall at one end of the patio. It was waist high and she sat down, still keeping her eyes focused on the wonderful display of stars. There was little doubt in her mind that New Mexico could be a land of enchantment at night. It seemed almost impossible that she was here, miles from home, in a place so unlike Ohio in every way.

Slowly Lori's gaze shifted from the overhead sky to the land that spread beyond the patio. And she saw a strange light. At first she thought it might be the reflection of the moon on some object in the desert. Then the light moved and she knew that what she was seeing was no reflection.

There was someone out there in the dark. Someone walking away from the Crying Winds. Whoever it was, was headed toward some rocky formation that stood eerily in the distance. The pueblo ruins. That's what it had to be.

Lori watched with curiosity as the light flickered and died away when whoever was carrying it came to the ruins. She wondered why anyone would be visiting that old place so late at night. Surely, this was no time to look for treasure.

Suddenly, Lori did not want to be out here alone on the patio. She slipped off the wall and hurried inside her room, locking the glass doors behind her.

Flicking off the light, Lori crawled into bed, drawing the covers up to her chin. Her head on the pillow was at an angle where she could still see the night sky.

Only, she wasn't thinking about the beauty of the night any longer. Her thoughts were on the mysterious light she had seen. Could the person she had seen be the same one who had worn the mask earlier that evening?

The crying winds moaned throughout the house like voices warning her of danger.

CHAPTER FIVE

Despite the things that had happened to her since she arrived at The House of the Crying Winds, Lori did sleep. It was uninterrupted by nightmares and she awoke refreshed.

The warm rays of the morning sun fell across her bed as she sat up, glancing around at the still unfamiliar surroundings. Then the memory of where she was swept over her, and she sprang out of bed and dressed.

As she hurried into the dining room, she smelled the tantalizing aroma of coffee being brewed.

"Good morning, Aunt Hannah," she said cheerfully when she entered the kitchen.

Her aunt nodded. "Did you sleep all right?"

"Fine, thanks. This New Mexico air certainly agrees with me. What can I do to help?"

Her aunt once again asked her to set the table, which Lori willingly did. Then she toasted some English muffins while Aunt Hannah scrambled eggs.

"Something odd happened last night before I went to bed," Lori said as she filled a small platter high with the muffins.

"You still going on about that mask? Like I told you, it was just somebody's idea of a joke."

"This happened later. I went out on the patio to look

at the sky and I saw a light. It was coming from the direction of the ruins, and it was really eerie."

Aunt Hannah went on with her work. "You mean the pueblo? That's crazy. Who would be going over there? Especially after dark. It's dangerous enough during daylight hours."

Lori could tell it had been a mistake telling her aunt about what she had seen. Now that it was broad daylight, it sounded just plain silly to talk about eerie lights. It sounded like a skittery, imaginative schoolgirl.

"I guess I was mistaken," Lori said, and Aunt Hannah appeared to accept that.

When Lori took the muffins into the dining room, Rex was there along with Oscar T. Owens.

"Good morning, Lori. How was your first night at the Crying Winds?" Rex asked, a wide grin on his handsome face.

"Just fine."

Oscar T. Owens excused himself, saying he had to make a phone call. When he was gone, Lori said, "I've got to talk to you, Rex. It's about something I saw last night."

"Go ahead. We're alone," Rex said.

"Just before I went to bed, I went out on the patio. I saw a light in the distance. It moved in the direction of the pueblo—at least, I think it was the pueblo—and then it was gone."

Rex listened intently. "A light, you say. Are you certain?"

"Of course. I tried to tell Aunt Hannah about it, but she isn't the easiest person to confide in."

"I wouldn't tell anyone else about what you saw," Rex said. "Not for the time being. I'm going out to the pueblo today and I'll look around."

"You do believe me, don't you?" Lori asked. "I wasn't just making that up about seeing the light."

"Certainly I believe you. I'll let you know what I find out."

They were interrupted by Isabel Jessop and the Neeleys, who entered the dining room. Isabel was talking up a storm, so Lori slipped away into the kitchen to help her aunt.

Breakfast turned out to be pleasant and brief. In the kitchen, as she was doing the dishes, Lori was told of her duties by Aunt Hannah.

"I'll handle the guest rooms," the older woman said. "You keep the living room and dining room in good shape. And you can take all calls. I'll do my own room. And you fix most of the meals. I'll do everything else. Do you think you can handle all that?"

Lori assured her aunt that she could.

"If it gets to be too much, you let out a holler," Aunt Hannah said in that no-nonsense voice of hers. "Anytime you want to return to Ohio, don't feel bad about telling me.

"But, Aunt Hannah," Lori said, "you were the one who wrote Father asking for help. Why is it so hard to get anyone to work here at the Crying Winds anyway?"

Aunt Hannah's eyes swept over Lori. "Appears to me you could figure that one out for yourself. Look around. There isn't anything for miles and miles. Guess it's just too isolated for most people. They'd rather work in Santa Fe or Albuquerque."

Since Aunt Hannah appeared to be in a talkative mood, Lori thought she would press on.

"Tell me about your childhood and Father's. Was it a happy one?"

Aunt Hannah stiffened. It was as though an invisible curtain had been dropped between the two of them. "Some other time, Lori. I have work to do on the patio."

Without a backward glance, Aunt Hannah walked purposefully out of the kitchen. Lori's feelings were a mixture of hurt and confusion. She had thought Aunt Hannah would want to talk about her only brother and their life together as children.

Even Aunt Hannah could not be so hard that she refused to discuss her childhood. Apparently, she was, Lori thought as she dipped her hands into the sudsy water. Then again, maybe it had been her timing. It was just possible that she had not gained Aunt Hannah's trust yet.

Lori might be rushing things. After all, the entire summer lay ahead of her. By the time summer had ended, she felt she and Aunt Hannah would be good friends. Just don't rush things, Lori said to herself.

When she finished in the kitchen, Lori went into the living room-office and began dusting. She had a transistor radio on and was concentrating on the music as she worked.

Lori became aware of the presence of someone else in the room before she actually saw Nancy Neeley.

The disagreeable woman was standing by the registration desk, and Lori got the feeling that Nancy Neeley had been there for some time watching her.

"You surprised me, Mrs. Neeley. Aunt Hannah asked me to clean up in here. Is there anything I can do for you?"

Nancy Neeley shook her head firmly. "Nothing. Unless you've seen my husband. I'm looking for him."

"Not since breakfast," Lori said. "If I do see him, I'll be glad to give him any message."

"There is no message. I was merely curious if he was here."

Lori faced down the hard stare of Nancy Neeley, who finally turned and left the room. If it wasn't for the fact that her Aunt Hannah was making money from these people, Lori would certainly have wished that the Neeleys would leave.

By the time Lori had finished cleaning the living room and the dining room and taken a few calls at the desk, it was approaching eleven o'clock. She went into the kitchen and prepared a platter of cold cuts and cheeses.

Then she made some potato salad and hurried into the dining room and set the table. She could not believe that the morning had gone so quickly. She had worked hard, but it had been fun.

Lori was just putting the food on the table when Aunt Hannah came in, followed by Oscar T. Owens.

"How about that! Not only is your niece a looker, but she's quite a cooker, too," Oscar T. Owens said and laughed uproariously at his own humor.

Aunt Hannah pretended she hadn't heard what the beefy salesman had said. "Looks mighty good, Lori," the older woman remarked. "Perfect food for a warm afternoon."

As if by instinct Isabel Jessop came in with a flourish, followed by the silent and mysterious Ray and Nancy Neeley.

"A buffet! How divine!" said Isabel.

The actress was wearing a filmy green caftan, and when she gestured, the garment appeared to take on a life of its own. Even the stoic Neeleys were caught off guard by Isabel's histrionics.

"This reminds me of the time I was on location in South America." Isabel had launched into another story.

At that moment Rex Fraser came into the room. Lori forgot all about the actress when she saw the tall blond giant.

"Everyone take your seats. That includes you, Aunt Hannah," Lori said, interrupting Isabel. "I'll get the rolls and butter. Please go on, Miss Jessop. Sorry to interrupt."

"Let me help," Rex said as he caught Lori by the arm and escorted her into the kitchen.

As Lori piled the warm rolls into a lined basket, Rex

said, "How was your first morning at Crying Winds?"

"Unbelievable. I've never worked so hard in my entire life, and enjoyed it so much. Aunt Hannah is doing the guests' quarters, and I'm in charge of the office and the dining room."

Rex laughed. "You talk as though this were your first job."

"It is. Believe it or not. Dad couldn't see me working. And since I always got a healthy allowance, there wasn't any point in working. But this is different."

"I wonder how you'll feel about the job at the end of the summer."

"That's a long time away. Right now I'm enjoying every minute. And besides that, I'm getting paid for what I do."

Rex grinned. "You may not know this, Lori, but outside of your sheltered world, that is the accepted thing. People expect to get paid for what they do."

Lori tossed a roll at Rex, which he expertly caught. She couldn't be angry at him. "I know you think I'm just playing at this job, but I'm not. I really want to help Aunt Hannah out."

"I know a way you can do that right now."

"How?"

"By taking those rolls into the dining room. There's a hungry bunch of drovers at that there chuckwagon."

They both laughed, and Rex opened the door leading to the dining room with excessive politeness. Lori picked up the tray with the rolls and butter, and she walked through the door.

Lunch was brief and lighthearted. This was mainly due to Oscar T. Owens and Isabel Jessop, neither of whom ever seemed at a loss for words.

As usual, the Neeleys were reserved and only spoke when asked a direct question. Aunt Hannah was not too talkative, but Lori couldn't help noticing that she always paid particular attention when Oscar had the floor.

After the dishes had been done, Lori wandered into the living room where Aunt Hannah met her. Her aunt was carrying some neatly wrapped bundles. There were more bundles on one of the couches.

"I still have some cleaning to do in number 8, Lori. The Neeleys are a demanding bunch. Would you mind counting and putting these towels and sheets away while I'm gone?"

"I'm here to help," Lori said with enthusiasm.

Her aunt showed her where the things should be put away and said, "No big rush. Relax a while. After all, I don't want you going back to your father with all kinds of tales about how I worked you to death."

Lori watched her aunt hurry off. Aunt Hannah had amazing vitality for someone her age. Her step was quick and sure. One thing surprised Lori, though. For a person who had spent her lifetime in the outdoors, Aunt Hannah's face and hands showed very little evidence of being weather-beaten. Particularly Aunt Hannah's hands which, although strong-looking, were quite feminine and well cared for. Apparently, Aunt Hannah at least had not abandoned her vanity.

After Aunt Hannah had gone, Lori fixed herself a cup of coffee and went out on the patio. The sky was a glorious blue, and the sun was a burnished medallion. She could see for miles. The visibility was incredible. In the distance loomed the mountains. A warm wind ruffled her tawny hair.

Lori found a lounging chair and settled down to enjoy the view.

She wondered where Rex was at this moment. He had told her that he intended going to the pueblo. There had been no mention of this at lunchtime, so she assumed that he hadn't had a chance to go there.

Idly Lori asked herself who might have been prowling

around the pueblo so late at night. Could that person have been the same one who had tried to frighten her with the mask?

What was there in the old ruins to attract anyone? It had been Rex who had spoken about the turquoise which had been left behind by the Indians. Was that only a story, or was there really a fortune buried in the old ruins?

Hearing the front door open, Lori got to her feet and hurried inside the house.

"There you are," came the affected voice of Isabel Jessop. "I've just taken a short walk. Would it be a bother to fix me a cup of coffee?"

"Not in the least. I was just having one myself. Why don't you join me on the patio?"

Lori realized this might be a strange way for the help to talk to a paying guest. But it had already been established that a certain informality—a certain blurring of distinctions—was the accepted thing here.

Lori walked into the kitchen and poured a cup of coffee for Isabel. When she returned to the patio, the actress had characteristically taken Lori's lounge chair. With an ironic smile Lori handed Isabel her coffee, then picked up her own cup and sat on a wrought-iron chair next to Isabel. Of course, she is the guest, Lori reminded herself. And I only work here.

"Pet, did I take your seat? Forgive me."

With Isabel that was easy to do. Lori noticed a dog-eared scrapbook inside the tote bag that the actress had with her.

"By now you must have some opinions on New Mexico and the Crying Winds," Isabel said. "Tell me everything."

"At first I didn't like New Mexico. It's so different from Ohio. Yet it has a certain beauty. Particularly the sunset. As for Crying Winds, I'm certain I'm going to like working for my aunt."

"Hannah Hudson can be a difficult person at times. But she's basically a good egg."

Lori took a sip of coffee. She did not wholly believe that Isabel Jessop was sincere. Still, with an actress, it was difficult to tell when she was playing a role or being herself.

"Is that your scrapbook? I couldn't help but notice," Lori said.

Isabel lighted up like a Christmas bulb. "Would you care to see it? Of course, most of the pictures are quite ancient. But nostalgia is still pretty big these days."

With that Isabel took out and opened the battered scrapbook and began explaining the pictures and the roles she had played. Lori found that the pictures consisted mainly of stills of Isabel. A much younger Isabel Jessop.

It was difficult for Lori to tell if the photographs she looked at were of the same person who reclined next to her. If there were others in a picture, they were so blurred as to be almost indistinguishable. Lori had to take Isabel's word that she was actually seeing Spencer Tracy, Franchot Tone, Cary Grant, and other luminaries.

After Lori had expressed her appreciation, Isabel quickly recovered the scrapbook and held it tightly under one arm.

"At the present I'm between roles. Any day I'm expecting a call from my agent. There is a pilot film in the works for some television series."

"What a fascinating life you must lead. What on earth are you doing at the Crying Winds?"

Lori noticed a slight stiffening in Isabel's manner. "It suits my purposes. I once was on location in New Mexico. I found the climate agreeable. Although I can't see why a young girl like you would want to come here."

"I wanted to help my aunt. And I wanted to get to know her better."

Isabel took a sip of the coffee. Then her watery eyes seemed to bore into Lori's. "If you were smart, you would catch the first bus out of here."

Lori gasped. "What are you saying?"

"Merely that the episode with the mask was just a warning. Whoever tried to frighten you must have had a reason. And I for one do not think that it was just a practical joke. Somebody obviously doesn't want you here at the hotel."

"I'm not afraid. That was a childish, foolish prank. And it'll take more than that to drive me away from here."

Isabel's eyes never left Lori's face. "I warned you."

CHAPTER SIX

"You can't be serious!" Lori said incredulously.

Isabel laughed then. "Don't pay any attention to me. I'm just being dramatic. You know us show-business people. Always overreacting to a situation."

"To what situation?" Lori said.

"Just circumstances. Do you know that you are not the only one who has had mysterious things happen to them since arriving at Crying Winds?"

Lori leaned closer.

"The evening I arrived, someone stole my makeup kit," Isabel said. "It was in the back seat of my car and I forgot to lock the door. Why on earth anyone would want that is beyond me."

"Did you report the theft to the police?"

"Of course not. After all, it was negligence on my part. They would only have told me that I should never leave my car unlocked. Which is true. Fortunately, I have two makeup kits, so it was no great loss to me."

Lori reached for her cup and took a sip of coffee. "Does Aunt Hannah know about the missing makeup kit?"

Isabel shook her head. "No. And I'm not about to tell her. She has her hands full as it is. Besides, the kit is gone. What good would it do to get her all stirred up over it now?"

"I suppose you're right. But tell me. Do you feel there might be some connection between the missing makeup kit and the prowler?"

"I didn't say that. However, I wouldn't take the matter too lightly. Not after what I told you."

Isabel finished her coffee and got to her feet. "I must be going. It's time for my siesta. I adore New Mexico's nights and mornings, but I can do without all this sunlight."

After Isabel had gone, Lori sat for a time thinking about what the actress had told her. Not only was there a prowler at Crying Winds, but a thief as well. Why would anyone bother taking a makeup kit?

Lori knew that in this day and age all kinds of things were stolen. It could have been someone who needed some quick cash, and the makeup kit was the first thing they laid their hands on. Still, it seemed odd. And who could the culprit be?

Lori found it impossible to imagine the theft being committed by anyone at the hotel. They all appeared to be quite well off financially, if not affluent. Still, appearances could sometimes be deceiving. She realized that she knew absolutely nothing about any of the guests. Only what they had told her.

Isabel Jessop could very likely be an actress, as she claimed. Only, Lori was not convinced, even after seeing the woman's scrapbook. The pictures could have been fakes. The young girl in them could have been a real actress—but not Isabel Jessop.

Even though Isabel had told Lori that the makeup kit had been stolen, how did she know the woman was telling the truth? She had said that she hadn't reported the theft to the authorities. So there was no way of confirming the incident.

Lori took a sip of coffee. It had grown cold and was bitter tasting.

Then there was Oscar T. Owens. A loud, coarse man who claimed to be a salesman. With his personality, Lori could imagine the man selling air-conditioning to an Eskimo.

Nancy and Ray Neeley were something else again. Of all the people at the Crying Winds, they were the most difficult to know. Lori wondered what business Ray Neeley had been in which would pay him enough retirement income to entitle him and his wife to drive all around the country. They were a mysterious, withdrawn couple, capable of doing anything.

Next, Lori's thoughts turned to Rex Fraser. He was the one person at the hotel she felt she could trust. The big blond giant was open and honest. There was no comparison between Rex Fraser and Blaine Edwards. Rex was forceful but considerate. Blaine was too self-indulgent and a trifle too immature. In a way, she was glad she had broken off with Blaine before she came to New Mexico.

Lori took the cups inside to the kitchen, where she rinsed them and stacked them on a drainer. Then she prepared a roast and put it in the oven for the evening meal.

The kitchen door opened and Rex Fraser walked in with a camera slung over one shoulder and a tripod in his right hand.

"I've been looking all over for you."

Lori smiled at the big handsome man. "You should have known that the kitchen is practically my home away from home."

Rex leaned the tripod against the wall and straddled a chair. "No need to ask how you're doing. You seem to know your way around a kitchen."

"Thank you. Have you been to the pueblo yet? We never got a chance to discuss it at lunch."

Rex shook his head. "Something came up and I had to delay going there. I was thinking about going out there in an hour or two. Would you be free to come with me? It would give you a chance to see a little of the countryside."

The idea appealed to Lori. "I'd love to go. Aunt Hannah won't mind, I'm sure. The house is cleaned and the roast is in the oven. All I have left to do is count and put away the linens in the hall closet."

"There will still be plenty of daylight in an hour or two so we'll be able to move around the pueblo freely. I wouldn't want to be caught in that place after sundown without a flashlight."

"Is it dangerous?" she asked.

"The place has been abandoned for years, so it has its share of holes and stumbling blocks. Not to mention all the damage that's been done by vandals and people searching for the lost treasure."

At the mention of the seekers of the lost treasure, Lori said, "I wonder if one of them could have been the person I saw last night. Do you think anyone would be so inquisitive that they would look for the treasure by flashlight?"

"It's possible. The lure of money does crazy things to some people. Only, I have a hunch that whoever you saw wasn't out there looking for buried treasure."

"Why was he out there? What other reason could there be?"

"It's only a hunch. I can't explain it. Maybe I'm mistaken."

Lori studied Rex's face for any sign of deception, but there was none. He just appeared to be thinking deeply about something he wasn't quite certain of himself.

"Did you know that Isabel Jessop's makeup kit was stolen the night she arrived here?"

Rex shook his head.

"She was with me earlier and told me all about it. It seems she left the car unlocked and the kit was in the back seat. When she went to check on it, the kit was gone. But she decided not to report it or anything."

"Why would anyone want to steal a makeup kit? It couldn't have been that valuable."

"Do you think there might be any connection between the theft and the prowler wearing the ceremonial mask?" Lori asked.

"It's possible. Why didn't Isabel report the crime to the police?" Rex asked, shifting his weight in the chair.

"She said something about it being her fault, not locking the car. And she was certain the police would feel the same way."

"That's true," Rex said. "Only, she should have reported it anyway. The police want to know about such things. You'd be surprised at the number of crimes that go unreported."

Lori hadn't thought about it, although she felt certain Rex knew what he was talking about.

"I'd better be going," Rex said, getting to his feet. "There are a lot of good shots to be taken while there's still daylight."

Lori hated to see him go because she enjoyed his company. She had never met anyone she could talk with so openly.

After he had gone, Lori stood at the kitchen window until she saw him trudging across the desert landscape. He must have sensed her presence because he turned and waved back at the house. Lori returned the wave, not certain if Rex had seen her or not.

Now that he was gone, she had to kill some time until he returned to take her to the pueblo. Then she remembered she had told Aunt Hannah she would count and put the towels and linens away.

Aunt Hannah had taken her into a hallway that was

behind the registration desk. The linen closet was a small, airless room with a single light, which, Lori found, to her consternation, had burned out. There were shelves that reached from the floor halfway up the wall. And the towels and bed linens were arranged in neat rows.

On an empty section of shelf, Lori saw a clipboard with a pencil attached on a dirty, frayed piece of string. She studied the top sheet of paper for a few minutes to decipher how Aunt Hannah had been keeping track of the laundry.

She was amazed when she discovered that there hadn't been an entry made on the tally sheet for a month or longer. But Aunt Hannah had been so busy, she probably hadn't had the time to keep it up to date. Lori wondered if the bookkeeping at Crying Winds was also in such neglected shape.

The laundry was wrapped in blue paper, and Lori took all the bundles into the hallway. The linen-closet door had a latch that locked from the outside. Woe to anyone who got locked inside, Lori thought. They would never get out!

She really should mention this safety hazard to Aunt Hannah. Beyond the door and down the hallway was another door which Lori assumed opened to the outside of the house. There was still so much of the hotel that she hadn't seen. Still, she was in no hurry to find out. After all, she had a good two months or longer to explore every nook and cranny.

Lori broke the twine on one of the bundles and sat on the floor to count and tally the sheets and towels. As she worked in the shadowy hallway, she felt that she was being watched. Every now and then she glanced around to reassure herself that she was alone. Even though she did not see anyone, the feeling that eyes were watching her still remained.

The old house was quiet; not even the sound of the wind

disturbed the solitude. A slight shiver went down Lori's spine in spite of the fact that it was the middle of the afternoon.

Once she thought she saw a shadow on a glass pane in the far door. Lori got to her feet and cautiously walked down the hallway. Then she slowly opened the door. When she looked outside, she only saw blinding sunlight. As she blinked away the glare, she looked in both directions, but there was nobody skulking around in that section of the yard.

"You're letting yourself get spooked," Lori muttered half aloud as she shut the door once again.

Even though she had seen no one outside, she still could not rid herself of the feeling that she was being observed. She knew that her uneasiness was prompted by her experience the previous night. Lori wondered how long the memory of that hideous face staring at her through the window would remain with her.

She had better put all that out of her mind, she told herself, and concentrate on getting the laundry put away. After all, she had promised Aunt Hannah that she would have it all done before dinner. Also, Rex should be coming by for her in a short while, and she wanted to be ready to go with him to the pueblo.

Suddenly, Lori was anxious to get out of the house, to be in the openness of the outdoors. She wanted to see the pueblo and perhaps find some trace of the mysterious person who had gone there so late last evening.

The linens and towels had all been unwrapped and counted and listed on the tally sheet. Lori leaned the clipboard against the wall, then gathered up an armload of towels and walked into the dark closet.

She had to stand on tiptoe to reach the area where the towels were kept. Sliding them into place, she hurried back for another armload. The closet was one place she didn't choose to stay in for too long a time.

As she was hastily arranging the next batch of towels, some fell to the floor. Lori squatted down to pick them up. While she was focusing her attention on the towels, the door slammed shut behind her. There was an unmistakable click as the lock on the door was turned. Then there were footsteps—footsteps walking away from the closet.

Immediately Lori arose from her crouching position and fumbled in the dark to get her bearings. Touching the door, she ran her hands down its smooth surface until she reached the doorknob.

She knew even before she tried it that the door would not open. The knob turned ineffectively under the pressure of her hand. Then Lori began to pound on the door. The sound was muffled in the quiet of the closet.

"Let me out! Somebody! Help me!" Lori heard herself cry out.

She was becoming panicky in the darkness, and her lungs filled up with the stale air. As she stood there, taking in gulps of air, she thought she heard footsteps outside the door. The sound receded as though whoever it was, was leaving her alone in her distress.

It had been no accident, Lori thought. Someone had deliberately locked her in the closet. Someone who now was going away, leaving her trapped inside the airless room.

Lori knew she mustn't panic. There was only so much oxygen in the room, and she must conserve what little there was. Once again she tried the doorknob and at the same time she pressed her shoulder against the hard surface, applying as much pressure as she could in the vain hope that the door would give.

It was to no avail. The door would not budge.

"Someone will find me," Lori said aloud. "All I have

to do is wait. It'll just be a matter of time."

Lori slumped to the floor, leaning her back against the wall. It was so dark she couldn't see her knees, which she had drawn up close to her chin. Her fear was slowly being replaced by anger. Whoever had done this might have thought it was an amusing trick. Only, Lori could see no humor in what had happened.

She didn't know how long she sat there, but slowly she began to grow sleepy. This frightened her because she knew it was due to the lack of oxygen.

Frantically, Lori got to her feet and began to pound on the door with what little strength was left in her body. She opened her mouth to cry out, but that seemed such a waste of effort. The effort at pounding on the door had drained her of her strength.

Lori leaned against the door for support. One stubborn hand continued feebly to strike the unyielding surface of the door.

Then it was no longer necessary. She was not aware of the clicking noise, nor of the door slowly opening. But suddenly there was a rush of fresh air, and she stumbled into Rex Fraser's arms.

CHAPTER SEVEN

Lori clung to Rex and his strong arms cradled her against his massive chest.

It was only after she began to breathe easier that he said, "Are you all right? Can you tell me how you managed to lock yourself in there?"

"I didn't. While I was putting some linen away, someone shut the door and locked it."

"Did you hear or see who might have done it?" Rex asked, holding her at arm's length.

"All the time I was in the hall, I had the feeling I was being watched. Even though I couldn't see anyone, the feeling was still there."

Rex looked at her thoughtfully with his brown eyes. "It's possible you were just imagining that. And it's also possible that the door closed on its own and somehow the lock fell in place."

Lori looked at him with disbelieving eyes. "Come on, Rex. How could that door close by itself? There wasn't a breath of wind. And—sometime before—I did see a shadow at the other door. By the time I got to the other door, though, whoever it was had gone. Besides, I heard footsteps walking away from the closet."

"Then you believe that someone deliberately locked you in the closet? But why?"

"For the same reason they tried to frighten me last night with the mask. Whatever reason that was."

"At least you're all right," Rex said as he led Lori out of the hallway into the living room.

"I feel fine. Only, if I'd stayed in there a little while longer, I wouldn't be so sure. If you hadn't come by when you did—"

"Don't think about it," Rex said as he and Lori sat down on a sofa. "I'd forgotten a filter for my lens. When I found it in my room, I decided to check on you. That's when I found the piles of laundry and the door locked. It's a good thing I decided to check on you."

Lori looked gratefully into Rex's face. Worry lines had formed between his thick, wheat-colored eyebrows.

"I don't suppose you feel up to going to the pueblo after what's happened to you," he said.

"Of course, I do. I've been looking forward to it ever since you asked me."

"That's the spirit. I like the way you bounce right back."

They both got to their feet.

Then Lori said, "Would you go with me while I finish putting the linens away? It's going to take some time before I'll feel safe going in there again."

"Just try and get rid of me," Rex said as he put his arm around Lori's shoulders.

Lori did not feel that he was being forward in his actions. As a matter of fact, she liked the feel of his strong arm around her.

It only took Lori—with Rex's help—a short time to stack the linens. Then they slipped out a side door and headed in the direction of the pueblo. The sky was a deep blue, the vastness broken by a few cotton-ball clouds. Lori took a deep breath of the clear, fresh air.

"Do you realize this is the first time I've been outside Crying Winds since I arrived?" she said as they walked along a narrow pathway, which was flanked by creosote bushes and mesquite.

"You'll find it's quite a change from Ohio," Rex replied.

"Have you been there? To Ohio, I mean."

"Once or twice. I get around in my business. So far I've been to about every state except Alaska and Hawaii."

"That must be exciting, traveling all the time."

Rex shrugged. "At first it was. Only, now I think I'd like to share it with somebody."

Lori didn't know what to say to that remark, so she kept silent. Rex was obviously a very sensitive person. That must be partly why he was such a good photographer, she reasoned.

Occasionally, Lori glanced over her shoulder at the hotel, which lay behind them. It was such a big, sprawling place, no wonder the original owner wanted to part with it.

Aunt Hannah had her hands full running the place. Fortunately, only a few rooms were occupied. With little or no advertising, Lori was amazed that even these few people had heard of the Crying Winds.

"What do you think of the Neeleys?" Lori asked as they trudged along.

"They're a strange couple," Rex said. "Keep to themselves a lot. In all the time I've known them, I don't think I've ever seen either one of them smile."

"Do you think it's possible that either one of them might have locked me in the closet?"

"It's possible. Only, what would be the reason behind it?"

"There isn't any," Lori said with a sigh. "For that matter, there wouldn't be any reason for anyone at the hotel to do it."

"Unless there is a hidden motive. Maybe one of them has a grudge against you."

Lori cast a quick sidelong glance at Rex. "That's not possible. I never even met any of those people back there until yesterday."

After that, neither one of them spoke as they drew nearer to the pueblo. Now, when Lori glanced around, she saw that the pueblo was built on a slight knoll. The ascent had been so gradual that she had not been aware of the climb until they were practically on top of the pueblo.

"We're here. But it's so unexpected," Lori said.

"The Indians built it out of adobe, so that it blends in with its surroundings," Rex said as he surveyed the ruins standing before them. "From what I've been able to garner, there were two main clans of Indians here. One was the summer or squash people, and the other, the winter or turquoise people. Some of them are still around. I'm told their corn festival is something to behold."

Lori had been listening raptly as Rex spoke. She could visualize the now dead village alive with people.

"I'd love to see the festival. When do they hold it?"

"In August. That's a long time away. No telling whether either of us will still be here by then."

Lori brushed a strand of tawny hair away from her eyes. "I don't know about you, but I plan to be here in August. And I plan on seeing the corn festival."

"You are a stubborn one. Your emerald eyes flash when you get your back up."

Lori stared at Rex in wonderment.

"Why are you looking at me that way?" he asked.

"You're the first person who ever called them emerald— besides my mother—not just green. She sort of has a thing about that. Always teasing me about it."

"They were the first thing I noticed about you, especially since your aunt has the same color eyes."

Lori shrugged. "It runs in the Hudson family."

"A very pleasing trait," Rex said as he took Lori in his

arms. "Up close they're even more lovely."

Rex kissed her gently and tenderly then. It was unexpected, but Lori found herself responding. Then, when the kiss ended, she said, "I thought we had come here to see the pueblo."

Rex grinned. "So we have. Let's look around. But watch your step."

The pueblo had been two stories high at one time. The ravages of time and vandals had reduced it to a single-storied grouping of jagged-edged buildings. As Lori walked cautiously through the ruins, she felt sad that this once thriving village was now nothing but a ghost town.

Moving through the ruins, Lori noticed that the earth was splotched with footprints. If the late-night prowler had come here, there would be no way of distinguishing his or her footprints from all the rest.

Rex was surprisingly well informed about the pueblo. He showed Lori where the corn was ground and a place where jewelry and pottery were undoubtedly made by the craftsmen of the pueblo. He found some broken shards to substantiate what he was saying.

"Even as dilapidated and run-down as it is, there is still something enchanting about the place," Lori said.

"The Indians have a chant that goes something like 'May it be beautiful all around me.' That certainly applies to New Mexico."

Lori looked at the sky and the surrounding countryside. New Mexico had cast its spell of enchantment on her. She knew that part of that enchantment was due to Rex Fraser. He made the whole experience exciting and interesting.

Suddenly, all that had happened to her at the hotel seemed like a dream. The prowler, the strange light in the night, and even the incident of the locked closet door all appeared to have happened to somebody else. Lori was glad she had come with Rex. She was beginning to lose her perspective staying in the hotel all the time.

They had come upon a wide, circular area in the center of what must have been the main thoroughfare of the pueblo. There was a crumbling, stunted wall surrounding the area.

"This was probably the kiva," Rex said. "Sort of a sacred place where the Indians met underground during their ceremonies."

"How interesting," Lori said, leaning over the wall. "Can we go down there?"

Rex shook his head. "I wouldn't advise it. Besides, it appears to be sealed off. I can't see any way that we can get to the underground passageways."

Lori was disappointed, yet she knew that Rex was right. It would be dangerous for them to try and enter the kiva even though she was filled with curiosity. From where she stood, she could see the surface of the kiva, which was covered with a fine layer of dust.

"Someone must have been curious about the kiva," Lori said to Rex. "Just look at all those footprints."

"Probably some vandal who didn't know any better."

"Or possibly someone looking for the buried turquoise," Lori said."

"That's possible."

Lori continued to look down at the kiva. She idly wondered if those footprints might belong to the person she had seen the night before. But she didn't express her thoughts to Rex. The footprints could have been made by vandals, after all.

They lingered at the kiva for a few more minutes while Rex explained how and when the ceremonial chamber was used. Lori listened with interest, marveling that Rex had done such extensive research on the pueblo.

"Where did you learn all that? Surely not from just talking to the local people."

Rex laughed. "Hardly. I try to do my homework before I go to a certain locale. That gives more meaning to the pictures. At least, it does for me."

"I agree. Your pictures are extraordinary. Each one of them seems to tell a story."

"Thank you. I value your opinion more than any editor's."

Lori laughed then. "You better stick with the editors. They're the ones who mail you all those nice little checks."

Then they both laughed as they turned away from the kiva. There was more of the pueblo that they hadn't seen, but it was getting late.

"Don't you think we should be heading back to the Crying Winds?" Lori suggested as they walked along the dusty street of the pueblo.

Rex glanced at his wristwatch. "You're right. I get carried away when I'm visiting some old ruins like this."

"If we don't get back, the roast will be an old ruin," Lori said with mock seriousness. "And I'm sure the guests at the Crying Winds wouldn't appreciate that."

"Nor your Aunt Hannah."

Lori grimaced. "Especially Aunt Hannah. All I have to do is make a mistake, and I get the feeling that I'll be sent packing back to Ohio."

Rex turned his gold-flecked eyes on Lori. "I hope that doesn't happen. At least not for a long time. I'm beginning to like your company, Lori Hudson."

Lori scanned Rex's face to make certain that he was serious. He was.

"I will have to confess that I find your company very interesting, too, Rex Fraser."

Rex pretended to be hurt by that remark. "Only interesting? After all I've done to make this outing as romantic as possible!"

Lori made an effort to ignore those words. "Now which

trail did we use getting here? They all look alike to me."

"I can see that you had better not go roaming about the countryside on your own," Rex said as he headed toward a well-worn path. He paused and turned toward Lori. There was a pleasant smile on his lips. "At this very moment I offer my services as your unofficial guide to New Mexico."

Lori laughed. "I accept. Now do you suppose my guide might be able to return me safely to the hotel?"

"If I can't, I'm not worthy of the name," Rex replied as he reached for Lori's hand.

Together they walked toward the Crying Winds. The afternoon sun was still bright. Lori shielded her eyes with her free hand and tipped her head forward so that she would not trip over the rock-strewn pathway.

She had given her hand to Rex so freely, so trustingly. The kiss he had given her back in the ruins was still fresh on her mind. There was little doubt now in Lori's mind that she was falling in love with Rex. Could this be? Could it happen in such a brief span of time?

All Lori knew was that she felt so good being around Rex that she had missed him when he had left her earlier that day. And how wonderful she felt when she had fallen into his arms after he had rescued her from the closet! Yes, she thought, love can happen in a few days or even a few hours, for that matter.

In a way she regretted having to leave the ruins and return to the Crying Winds. Something was wrong at the hotel. Only, Lori did not know what it was. Would the "accidents" continue once more when she returned?

Should she tell Aunt Hannah what had happened to her in the closet? Or would Aunt Hannah not believe her as she apparently hadn't when Lori had mentioned the light she had seen in the darkness? Lori sighed in confusion.

Glancing down, she saw a sudden flash of light as something on the path caught a ray of sunlight.

"Wait, Rex! I thought I saw something," Lori said as she paused and stooped down.

There, lying on the ground, was a small pin crudely shaped like a bird. Around its neck were some blue stones.

"It's a pin someone lost. What is it, Rex?"

Rex took the pin in his hand and studied it for a moment. "Looks like a bird carved from basalt. Unless I'm mistaken, those stones around its neck are turquoise."

"Turquoise!" Lori said. "Do you think this might be some of the buried treasure?"

"I doubt it. More likely somebody lost it while hiking. See how loose the clasp is on the back? It probably dropped off and the owner never knew it was gone. Looks as though you've found a trophy. Something to remember the ruins by."

Lori turned the odd-shaped bird over in her hands, then tucked it into a pocket.

"Maybe it belongs to someone at the Crying Winds. I'll ask around when we get back."

As they continued on their way, Lori wondered if the bird had any connection with the strange light she had seen the night before.

CHAPTER EIGHT

Aunt Hannah was waiting for Lori when she returned with Rex.

"You two been having fun?" she asked with a quizzical tilt of an eyebrow.

"We went for a walk," Lori hastened to explain. "I finished my work and I thought you wouldn't mind."

Aunt Hannah gave Lori what might pass for a smile. "Can't expect you to work all the time. Being a relative doesn't exactly make you a hired hand."

"It was my suggestion, Hannah," Rex said. "I didn't think you'd mind if I took your niece on a short tour."

Rex's winning ways were not lost on Hannah Hudson. It was obvious to Lori that her aunt liked the tall, bronzed giant.

"Don't mind in the least. Lots of good scenery to take in around these parts."

"We just went to the pueblo," Lori said. "I'd heard so much about the old ruins I just had to see it."

Aunt Hannah frowned. "The pueblo! There's nothing to see in that place. Wouldn't waste energy going to that pile of decaying adobe. I would prefer that you didn't go there again, Lori. It's too dangerous."

Lori did not like the tone of Aunt Hannah's voice. And she certainly didn't like being told she couldn't do something. But she did not feel like arguing at the moment.

Instead, she reached inside her pocket and brought out the pin that was shaped like a bird.

"We found this just as we were leaving the ruins. Someone must have dropped it."

Aunt Hannah gave the pin a quick flick of her attention. "There are probably hundreds of pins like this in New Mexico. It could belong to just about anybody."

Lori took back the pin. Aunt Hannah was probably right. It would be like looking for a needle in a haystack to try and find the owner.

"And it's just possible," Rex said, "that this pin could also belong to somebody here at the hotel."

Aunt Hannah looked questioningly at Rex. "What is so important about that pin?"

"It might explain a few things that have happened to me since I arrived here." Lori had spoken up before she realized what she had said.

"You mean that practical joke with the mask? Is that still bothering you?" Aunt Hannah asked, her mouth twisted into a faint sneer.

Lori felt she had to explain her last statement. "Not only that, but I did see someone at the ruins last night. And this afternoon somebody locked me in the linen closet."

"Locked in the linen closet! You sure do have a lively imagination." It was plain from the expression on Aunt Hannah's face that she did not believe Lori's story.

"I wasn't imagining it. If Rex hadn't come by when he did, I would still be in there."

Aunt Hannah sneered. "It must have been an accident. Probably the door just closed by itself and you thought somebody had locked you in."

"Aunt Hannah, you know that isn't true. That lock on the door is a hazard. And I did hear somebody in the hall after I got locked in. Somebody who walked away when I cried out for help."

"If you keep on with this, Lori, I'll have no other choice but to ask you to leave," Aunt Hannah said. "After all, I can't have you spreading such stories to the guests. This business is all I have and I intend keeping it."

With that Aunt Hannah went to her room. Lori was flabbergasted and somewhat hurt by her aunt's words.

"Do you think she meant that, Rex? That she would send me back to Ohio?"

Rex took Lori's hands in his. "She was just upset. I don't think she really meant what she said."

"All the same, I suppose she is right. It wouldn't do any good to tell the other guests what's happened to me. If the Crying Winds got a bad reputation because of something I said, I would feel terrible."

Rex smiled at her. "In that case we'll keep it a secret. Only, at the same time, we'll keep our eyes and ears open. I have a feeling that whoever is harassing you is staying here at the hotel. Who else could it be?"

"But why, Rex? I haven't done anything to the guests. It just doesn't make sense."

"All I know is that somebody wants you to leave in the worst way. And I want you to stay in the same way. I have my reasons."

"What are they?" Lori asked.

Rex didn't hesitate. "I've grown very fond of you, Lori. Can you believe that?"

Lori nodded her head. "I can. That's how I feel about you. Only, it all happened so quickly. I couldn't make myself believe that it could happen so fast."

"Darling," Rex said as he kissed Lori lingeringly, "you see now you can't leave Crying Winds. Not just yet, anyway."

Lori knew that Rex spoke the truth. If she had to leave the hotel before the summer was over, it would crush her.

Rex sniffed the air. "Do you smell something?"

"My roast!" Lori cried as she raced toward the kitchen. "I'll see you at dinner. If there is going to be any."

She heard Rex's faint laughter as she entered the kitchen. The roast was salvageable, although it would be a little dry; but a light gravy would take care of that. Lori peeled some potatoes and put them on the back burner to cook, then went to her room to shower and change for dinner.

As the cold pellets of water stung her body, she thought about what Aunt Hannah had said. It was almost as though her aunt was waiting for Lori to make a mistake or create a scene so that she would have the opportunity to ship her back to Ohio.

Lori couldn't have that. If she hadn't fallen in love with Rex, perhaps she wouldn't have minded so much. Then she thought about her mother and father. If Aunt Hannah made good her word to send her home, Lori knew how disappointed her parents would be. Not only that, she would have proved nothing in coming to New Mexico.

Lori dried herself on a towel and put on a green linen dress. Then she hurried into the kitchen where she slipped on an apron. Aunt Hannah came into the kitchen just as Lori had sliced the roast and set it in a bed of mashed potatoes.

"Didn't intend to sound off in front of Mr. Fraser," Aunt Hannah said. "And I didn't mean to embarrass you."

Lori knew this was as close as her aunt would ever get to apologizing.

"I understand. You were right. I probably have let my imagination run away with me. I won't say a word to any of the other guests about the closet."

Aunt Hannah appeared to be relieved. "That roast looks good. Got to admit you know your way around a kitchen."

Lori would not let her aunt help her with serving when she offered. "You hired me to do a job, and that's what

I intend doing. Now why don't you see to the guests? Dinner will be on the table in a few minutes."

"At least you got spunk," Aunt Hannah said as she walked out of the kitchen.

At dinner that night Lori watched the faces of the guests as they gathered around the big mahogany table. She had made a vow not to mention getting locked in the linen closet, but there was no way of preventing her from looking for something suspicious in the faces of the guests.

Oscar T. Owens was his usual bumptious self. And, as usual, it was a contest between himself and Isabel Jessop to see who would be the center of attention.

When both of them paused long enough to taste the roast, Lori said, "How did your sales go today, Mr. Owens?"

Oscar shrugged. "I didn't go out today. I'm behind in my paperwork. You'd be surprised at the pencil-pushing I have to do on my job."

So Oscar had been around all day. He could have very easily locked her in the closet. Yet when she looked at the jowly man, she could not believe that he was interested in anything other than talking and his business.

"Just what do you sell, Mr. Owens?" Isabel Jessop said in theatrical tones.

"That's for me to know and you to find out," Oscar replied, evading the question. "This roast is just the way I like it, Lori."

"A little too well-done for my liking," came the voice of Nancy Neeley. "But a pretty young thing like Lori isn't supposed to know too much about cooking."

Lori clenched her fists under the table. She made every effort not to let on that Nancy Neeley's remark had angered her.

In a cool voice, she said, "Perhaps you will tell me what

your favorite dish is, Mrs. Neeley. I would be happy to prepare it for you."

"I'm with Oscar," Rex said. "The roast is perfect."

"I have a feeling that might be because you like the cook," Aunt Hannah said wryly.

"Guilty," Rex answered, and there was a sound of laughter that eased the tension.

"Tell me, Rex," Isabel Jessop said after she had taken a sip of water, "did you get some good photographs today?"

Rex put down his fork and turned his gold-flecked eyes on the aging actress. "I believe I did. Earlier this afternoon. Then I didn't take my camera when Lori and I went to the pueblo."

Lori glanced nervously at her aunt, but Hannah Hudson did not appear to be upset at what Rex had said.

"Good for you," Isabel said with a dramatic lift of one hand. "You got that poor Cinderella out of the scullery for a while. But of all places! Why on earth did you go to those crumbling ruins?"

Rex was very tactful, much to Lori's relief. "The ruins have a lot of light and shadow, and they aren't too far from the hotel. I plan on taking a series of shots there. Both by daylight and night."

Isabel squirmed in her chair. "You won't get me to go to that creepy old place. Especially at night. Although we did do some night locations in Mexico for one of my pictures."

"That must have been one we missed," Ray Neeley said sarcastically. Then he turned to Rex. "Tell me, Mr. Fraser, is there any truth to the legend we've heard about a fortune in turquoise being buried at the pueblo?"

All eyes were turned on Rex, who nonchalantly took a sip of water before answering. "As far as I have been able to find out, the legend of the missing turquoise is just that. A legend. But that doesn't seem to keep some people from vandalizing the ruins in search of the turquoise."

Ray Neeley was not to be put off so easily. "You must admit that there had to be some basis for the story."

Rex nodded.

"In that case, it's a likelihood that there just might be some treasure hidden away somewhere in those old ruins," Ray Neeley said.

Aunt Hannah snorted. "If there was any truth in that old legend, somebody in all these years might have found something. It's just a lot of nonsense."

"I agree," Oscar T. Owens said. "Why anyone would waste their time and energy poking around some decaying adobe is beyond me. You'll find no treasure in that place."

"But you are mistaken, Oscar," Rex said, and Lori wondered what Rex was getting at. "Only this afternoon Lori found a rare pin. Zuni, I would say. So the afternoon wasn't a complete loss."

"A pin?" Isabel said anxiously. "What does it look like? Do you still have it, Lori?"

Lori nodded her head, stealing a quick glance at her Aunt Hannah.

Surprisingly Hannah Hudson said, "Why don't you show Miss Jessop the pin, Lori? The clasp is broken, but it's still in good shape."

With Aunt Hannah's sanction, Lori reached into the pocket of her dress where she had placed the turquoise bird. Then she handed it to Isabel Jessop, who exclaimed and enthused over it.

"Why, Lori, this is adorable. Such a quaint little bird."

Lori's eyes scanned the faces at the table for any telltale signs, but all she saw was curiosity on the faces of the guests. The pin obviously didn't belong to anyone present.

Or, if it did, whoever owned it was cleverly disguising his feelings.

"Looks as though you've gotten yourself a souvenir, young lady," Oscar T. Owens said, wiping his chin with his napkin. "If I could get hold of a gross of those, I wouldn't have any trouble in selling them."

Isabel reluctantly returned the pin and Lori once again tucked it away in the pocket of her dress.

Rex wandered into the kitchen while Lori was doing the dishes and, as he helped, they discussed what had transpired at dinner.

"From what I saw in their faces, I would say that the pin didn't belong to anybody at the hotel," Rex said, stacking the plates on the counter.

"Either that or they are all as good at acting as Isabel Jessop."

"You could be right. If the pin belonged to one of the other guests, they felt they couldn't let on. Otherwise, there might be some questions as to when they were at the pueblo."

Lori rinsed out the sink and dried her hands on a towel. "All we can do is suspect no one or everyone."

"That includes me," Rex said. "After all, I could very easily be the one who wore that mask. I did find it pretty quickly, you know. And I could have dropped the pin when I was searching the ruins last night."

Lori gave Rex an amused smile. "Did you?"

Rex shook his head. "No. I hope you believe me."

"I do. Of all the people at the Crying Winds, you're the only one I feel I can trust."

"Thanks. I'll try to live up to that. I just thought I would bring it up so that you knew where I stand. Like I said before, Lori, I'm beginning to like your company."

Lori knew that Rex was telling her the truth, so she

believed that he had not been the prowler nor the one who
had locked her in the linen closet. Even though Rex had
been the one who had found her, she could not believe
that he would have locked her in and then made a pretext
of discovering her.

He seemed so honest and truthful, she would never
believe that Rex would ever be anything other than what
he claimed to be.

Rex took her in his arms and held her close. He gently
brushed her lips with his own. Then they broke apart. She
looked around the kitchen.

"Just checking to make sure all the dishes have been
washed and put away," Lori said.

Rex laughed. "You really do plan on earning your keep
here, don't you?"

"That's why I came. Aunt Hannah said she would pay
a salary besides room and board. If I let her down, I'd be
doing the same to myself."

Rex helped her put away the last of the dishes. Then
he took her by the arm. "I guess we should join the others
in the living room."

Lori moved to his side. As they left the kitchen, she
touched the turquoise pin in her pocket and wondered if
it really belonged to someone at the hotel. And if so, to
whom?

CHAPTER NINE

Lori and Rex managed to slip into the living room unnoticed. Oscar T. Owens had the floor and was talking about the road conditions in Montana during the winter season. Everyone except Isabel Jessop was listening raptly.

Taking a seat on a sofa, Lori and Rex halfheartedly gave their attention to the beefy man. Lori observed that Oscar's glass of brandy was half empty. The man apparently liked his comforts.

Across from their sofa, the Neeleys sat primly aloof from the rest of the people. If anyone was capable of locking her in the linen closet, Lori felt the Neeleys were. Then Lori's gaze shifted to Isabel Jessop.

The orange-haired woman was looking at her nails, pretending not to be interested in what Oscar T. Owens was saying. Isabel was outwardly an actress.

Yet Lori wondered what went on inside the woman's head. It had been Isabel who had warned Lori to leave the Crying Winds. Had she gone a step further with her warning and been the one who had pressed the lock on the linen-room door before she had slammed it shut?

It was Aunt Hannah who called an abrupt end to the evening.

"It's been a long day. I'm turning in," she said, getting to her feet.

The abruptness of her gesture plunged the guests into an awkward silence as one by one they left the cozy atmosphere of the living room for their quarters.

"It's still early," Rex said to Lori after they had all gone. "Do you feel up to a breath of fresh air on the patio?"

"A wonderful idea. I'll get a sweater and be right with you," Lori said, hurrying to her room where she grabbed a sweater from a hanger in the closet.

The patio was cool with the ever-present crying wind moaning in the trees. Tonight Lori did not mind the eerie sound. With Rex at her side she was enjoying the wide expanse of sky with its sprinkling of brilliant stars.

Rex led her to a shadowy portion of the patio where there were two chrome chairs. They sat quietly, listening to the sound of the wind and the night noises of insects.

It was Rex who broke the silence. "Did you notice any suspicious looks when you showed Isabel that turquoise pin?" He couldn't leave the subject alone.

"None. Everyone appeared to be interested, but that was all. If it belonged to anyone at the table, they did a great job of hiding the fact."

"I agree. Of all the people that were at the table, the Neeleys seemed to be the most inquisitive. Ray was unusually interested in learning about the buried treasure. He ordinarily isn't a very talkative person."

"They are such a strange pair. What do you know about them, Rex?"

"Nothing much. From what I gather, he's retired. But you know that. Besides, it could just be a story. We only have his word for that."

"Do you think it's possible that he and his wife are here to find the buried treasure?"

Rex shifted in his chair. "It could very well be. He wouldn't be the first one who was lured here by the prospect of getting rich. Even if the story is just a legend."

"Then you really don't believe there is a buried treasure in the pueblo."

"I'm inclined to go along with what your Aunt Hannah thinks."

"But what about the turquoise bird? Couldn't that have been from the abandoned treasure?"

Rex shook his head. In the light cast by the full moon, the patio—aside from the dark portion they occupied—was almost as bright as day. "No. The pin must have dropped off while whoever wore it was exploring the ruins. There just doesn't seem to be any other explanation for it."

Lori felt that Rex seemed so sure that there was no treasure buried in the pueblo that she herself now had doubts. Like anyone new to the area, she found the story held a certain fascination. She had wanted to believe that the treasure existed. Therefore she had. Now there were doubts in her mind.

"What will you do when the summer is over and you return to Ohio?" Rex asked, changing the subject.

"Back to school. That's where I'll go. Only, right now I don't want to think about that. I've had enough schooling for a while. I just want to spend the summer doing something other than cracking a book."

"I can understand that," Rex said. "With all the work you have here at the hotel, I don't think you'll have time to think about college. And whatever free time you have, I want to be part of it."

Lori gazed at the blond giant who sat next to her. She suddenly wondered how hard it would be to say good-bye to him when the summer had ended. In the brief time she had known Rex Fraser, she had fallen in love with him. Yet she wondered now if that had been wise. Summer would ultimately come to an end and what then? Well, she would just have to cross that bridge when she came to it.

For now she was going to cherish all the time she had with Rex.

"What happens when you finish taking all the pictures you need?" Lori asked.

Rex was silent for a moment. "I'll be moving on. I have my assignments laid out for me. Wherever I'm told to go, I go. It's my job."

The freedom she thought Rex enjoyed did have certain restrictions, Lori reckoned. Even a freelance photographer apparently wasn't as free as the name implied.

"What got you interested in photography and cameras?" Lori asked.

"Ever since I was a kid I've had a camera slung around my neck. Now I've finally become a professional. But I haven't been at it very long. Then this offer to come to New Mexico came my way, and I couldn't refuse."

Lori had thought that Rex Fraser had been in the business a long time. Apparently, he just recently became a freelancer. She idly wondered how she had gotten the impression he had been in the business such a long time.

What had he done before he became a photographer? For the first time since their meeting, Lori realized she actually knew very little about the handsome man sitting next to her.

As she was about to ask him a question, someone came into the patio. Simultaneously she and Rex glanced in that direction. It was Ray Neeley. He had started toward the front gates of the hotel when he sensed their presence. He was carrying something in his right hand, and he thrust it into the pocket of his jacket.

"Just out for a breath of fresh air. I see I'm not the only one with that idea," he said as he strolled toward them.

"Yes, it's a lovely night," Lori said. "So much different than Ohio."

"Ohio. Never been there. Do you recommend it as a place to visit, Miss Hudson?"

Lori thought for a moment before answering. "It's my home state. And I'm used to it. Even though it's a lot different from New Mexico, it has its attractions."

"No doubt you are right. Perhaps someday my wife and I will be heading in that direction. As soon as my business is finished here."

"Just what sort of business is that?" Rex asked.

"Private business," was the cold reply. It was evident that Ray Neeley had no intention of telling more than he wished.

"How did you and your wife happen to come to the Crying Winds?" Lori asked.

"It was recommended to us by some friends."

"The hotel is quite isolated. Does that bother you at all?" Lori asked.

"It suits my purposes. My wife and I are not social people. The isolation of the hotel is very much to our liking. But I don't understand what two young people like you are doing here."

Lori waited for Rex to speak. When it became evident he wasn't going to answer the brusque man, she said, "My aunt needed some help for the summer. I thought the change from Ohio would be good for me."

"I see. And of course you have your photography, Mr. Fraser."

"That's right."

"You must forgive me for saying so, but I find that making a living with a camera a rather risky thing."

Rex said, "Everyone to their own opinion. At least I don't make a secret of my line of business."

Lori saw Ray Neeley outwardly flinch at the barb. It was very evident that there was no love lost between the two men.

"If you will excuse me, I must be getting back to my wife. Good night."

Turning on his heel, Ray Neeley walked briskly across

the patio, his footsteps snapping against the cold concrete.

"I think you upset the man," Lori said when Ray Neeley had gone.

"I doubt that. He's a cool one and that goes for his wife, too."

"I thought he was retired. But I suppose he still keeps in touch with his former business."

Rex shrugged and then Lori said, "He acted as though he was surprised at finding us on the patio. I wonder if he really came out for a breath of air?"

"Then you saw the flashlight he had in his hand. He was quick in shoving it in his pocket, but not fast enough."

"Do you suppose Mr. Neeley might have been the person I saw last night?" Lori asked.

"It's possible. That flashlight made him appear very suspicious. Especially the way he tried to conceal it. I think he intended going to the ruins, but when he saw us, he changed his mind."

Lori drew her sweater closer to her body. "But why would he be going to the ruins, especially at night? He couldn't possibly be looking for the treasure in the dark."

"Maybe there is another reason. Something that hasn't anything to do with the buried treasure. If we knew what he was looking for, we might have some answers to what's been happening to you."

"What do you mean?"

Rex reached out and took one of Lori's hands in his. "I mean the person who wore the mask to frighten you into leaving Crying Winds. And you were not accidentally locked in that closet today. Can't you see, Lori? Whoever wants you to go is becoming more desperate. The next time the accident might be harmful to you."

"Why does that person want me to leave? It doesn't make any sense. If I knew some terrible secret about the hotel, I could understand. But I don't have any idea why that person wants me to leave."

Rex held her hand more tightly. "Maybe it's not because of something you know. Perhaps it's because of something you might find out."

Lori shook her head, trying to fathom what Rex was saying. "If there is something going on here, something that might possibly harm Aunt Hannah, then I won't leave. And nobody is going to force me to."

Rex chuckled. "You are a stubborn one. I only hope that stubbornness doesn't get you into trouble. In the meantime, I want you to be on guard. Don't trust anybody. Watch whatever you do."

"You don't have to warn me. But I do appreciate your concern."

Rex stood up, bringing Lori to her feet at the same time.

"I am concerned about you."

He took her in his arms and his kiss was thoughtful and caring.

"I'd better go in now," Lori said, reluctant to leave his strong embrace and nevertheless certain that she should. "After all, I am a working person now."

Rex walked her inside, then headed for his own room.

The house creaked and moaned with the sound of the crying winds. Aunt Hannah was probably fast asleep.

Lori went to her room and undressed, then put on her pajamas and crawled between the covers. As she lay there, she thought about Aunt Hannah. Was the person who was doing these things to her trying to get to Aunt Hannah through her? What was the secret of The House of the Crying Winds and how did it involve her?

Sleep came gradually to Lori, and it was not restful. Her dreams were haunted by dark corridors and frightening shadows. She was alone in the corridors, but she felt she was being watched. The wail of the winds was like the crashing of angry waves against a rugged shoreline. As the sound grew louder, she began to quicken her steps. Now she knew that she was being pursued.

Lori awoke with a start and slowly the nightmare began to fade from her mind. She got out of bed and walked to the patio window. Standing there, she saw a flickering light in the faraway darkness. Then it was gone. Had she actually seen the light, or was it her imagination working overtime? With a shiver Lori returned to her bed. Sleep came quickly and she was not tormented with nightmares this time.

When she opened her eyes, it was light. She stretched and yawned and flung the covers from her body. In the warm light of day, it was impossible to believe the fears she had experienced during the night.

After she had taken a quick, bracing shower, Lori put on some jeans and a blue linen blouse. She ran a comb through her tawny hair and added a touch of gloss to her lips. For a moment she studied her reflection in the mirror. Then, with a nod of approval, she left the room.

Aunt Hannah was still in her room. She was obviously a late riser. That was understandable, Lori thought, since she worked so hard during the day.

Lori would have liked to help her aunt with the other rooms, but she had to tread carefully around Hannah Hudson. The wrong words might be the ones which would find her boarding a plane back to Ohio.

Lori arranged the table for breakfast. Then she went into the kitchen to get the breakfast started. As Lori gathered the cooking utensils, she thought about Rex.

In a short while they would be sitting together at the table. Somehow she would tell him about seeing the light again last night. It would have to be when the others were preoccupied.

And she knew that she would not dare mention a word

of what she had seen to Aunt Hannah. With a sigh, Lori felt that she was no closer to her aunt than she had been the day she arrived. Hannah Hudson was not an easy person to get to know. Even though she was a blood relative, she was almost a stranger to Lori.

When Lori opened the refrigerator to get the eggs and milk, her glance fell upon the plate which had held the leftover roast from the night before. The plate was still there, but the remainder of the roast was gone.

Someone had taken the meat during the night. It angered her at first that one of the guests had been so forward as to help himself to the refrigerator contents. Then the anger turned to concern.

Did this latest episode have anything to do with the strange events that had been happening at the hotel? And how did the person get to the kitchen? At night, the private quarters of Lori and her aunt—including the living room, dining room, and kitchen—were locked.

CHAPTER TEN

Although everyone at breakfast was in a good mood, Lori wondered which one, if any of them, had taken the food. Rex got away before she could talk to him, and then there was only Aunt Hannah and Oscar T. Owens at the table.

Hannah Hudson said, "We're getting low on supplies. How about you going shopping for me, Lori?"

"I'd be glad to. But what about my work?"

"I can handle that. Here's a list I made up. I usually buy things at the Big Five Market in Santa Inez."

Lori took the list along with the keys to one of the cars that were parked in the garage next to the hotel.

As she began to clear the table, Lori said, "Aunt Hannah, does anyone besides you and me have a key to our quarters?"

"What kind of question is that? Of course not. Why should they?"

"Last night I put the leftover roast in the refrigerator and this morning it was gone. Did you eat it, Aunt Hannah?"

"I can answer that," Oscar T. Owens said as Lori turned her attention to the jowly man. "Your aunt fixed me a sandwich last night for my lunch today. I'm planning to be away until late. Might not even make it for dinner."

Lori looked at her aunt. For a moment Hannah Hudson's

face seemed bewildered. Then, as quickly as it had come, the bewilderment vanished. "That's right. You must have been gallivanting around with Rex Fraser at the time."

Lori wasn't sure she knew what the word gallivanting meant, but she didn't like the sound of it. And she felt that her aunt had backed up Oscar T. Owens's story. There was no sense in pursuing the matter now; Aunt Hannah was definitely on Oscar's side.

After washing the breakfast dishes—Lori felt that was the least she could do to help her aunt—she went to her room to get her purse. The turquoise bird was lying on the chest of drawers and Lori unconsciously dropped it into the purse.

Before she went to the garage for the car, Lori decided that she would check to see if Rex was still in his room. He had warned her to be careful in what she did. She felt he would want to know about her trip to Santa Inez.

Lori rapped on the door of number 10 and waited. There was no sound from within. Then she rapped a second time, but Rex had obviously gone out with his camera. She was about to leave a note, then thought better of it. The note would be so obvious on the door that anyone could read it and find out where she was going.

Feeling somewhat uneasy, Lori walked to the garage and drove the car out and headed in the direction of Santa Inez.

The morning was fresh and the wind coming in from the open windows was balmy. Lori glanced in the rearview mirror to see the Crying Winds slowly receding in the distance.

She welcomed the chance to get away from the hotel for a while. She felt that no harm could come to her during the daylight hours.

It was a long drive to Santa Inez, as Lori remembered when Rex had driven it a few days before. She thought about how her feelings had changed toward him since she had first met him at the depot. How crude he had appeared then and how rudely she had treated him.

His first impression had been deceiving. She had fallen in love with this tall, blond giant of a man. Yet was that wise? She felt that Rex loved her, but he had never once said so. He had implied that he would miss her when the summer had ended. Did that mean that he intended going his way as she must hers?

A roadrunner skittered along the side of the road and disappeared into a clump of underbrush. Once again Lori was reminded of how different New Mexico was from her native state. When she had first arrived, she had almost despised the land. By now it had captured her with its stark beauty.

Topping a hill, she began to think about her Aunt Hannah. Such a cold, withdrawn woman. Lori had expected her aunt to be of an independent nature but not lacking in warmth. Hannah Hudson was still an enigma to her.

Then there were the other guests. Isabel Jessop, a vain, self-centered actress who might not be what she claimed to be. And Oscar T. Owens, the portly salesman whom Aunt Hannah appeared to like. Whatever her aunt saw in the obnoxious man was beyond Lori.

The Neeleys were definitely a strange couple. Lori wondered why Ray had hidden the flashlight from Rex and herself last night on the patio. He and Nancy were so mysterious in their actions and so aloof that they just naturally were suspicious people.

After that, Lori concentrated on her driving with an occasional glance out the window at the passing scenery.

When she arrived at Santa Inez, she stopped for gas and asked for directions to the Big Five Market. While she was waiting for the car to be refueled, she decided to call Bessie, the woman she had met on the bus.

"Lori! Are you all right?" Bessie asked excitedly when she answered the phone.

Lori could hardly keep from laughing at the woman's concern. "I'm fine. Aunt Hannah asked me to do some shopping for her. So I'm in town for a few hours. And I thought I would call you."

Bessie appeared relieved that Lori was not in some dire trouble. "Why don't you have lunch with us? Here at the house."

"If you don't think it would be too much trouble."

"My sister always cooks enough for Sherman's army. We'll just put another plate on the table."

Lori agreed. It would be nice to have lunch with Bessie and talk to her again. Besides, she wouldn't be expected to set the table and wash the dishes afterward.

The attendant was just finishing cleaning the windows when Lori came back to her car after talking to Bessie. She followed the directions he had given her and only got lost once before she found the market. Santa Inez was a pleasant little town, she realized.

After she had finished shopping, which took longer than she had anticipated, Lori glanced at her watch and saw that it was eleven o'clock. Asking directions Lori drove through the quiet little town until she found the street where Bessie was staying. The house was adobe and glistened whitely in the noonday sun.

Bessie was at the car door soon after Lori pulled into the driveway.

"Tell me everything that's happened, dear. I must say that New Mexico agrees with you. And fill me in on that photographer fella you talked about on the phone."

After putting the perishables in the refrigerator—Bessie's idea—Lori did her best to catch Bessie up on her experiences since arriving at the Crying Winds. Anita, Bessie's sister, made her feel at home.

The house was not expensively furnished but very warm and comfortable. Just as Lori had imagined the house that Bessie's sister lived in would look like. Lori found out that Anita's husband was a truck driver and was on a run, not expected back for a few days. The two children got over their initial shyness and accepted Lori as one of the family.

Anita had prepared enchiladas and frijoles with a crisp salad. Lori found that she was hungry and had seconds of everything. This pleased Anita, who obviously took pride in her culinary skills.

"Did I tell you, Bessie, that there is a movie star staying at the Crying Winds?"

Bessie said, "Yes, you did. What was her name again?"

"Her name is Isabel Jessop. Have you ever heard of her?"

Bessie conferred with Anita for a few moments, then said, "We're both great movie fans. But we've never heard of her. Still, that dosen't mean she isn't a star."

Lori was somewhat disappointed that neither Bessie nor Anita had ever heard of Isabel. She had hoped that they would remove any suspicion she had of the aging actress. Now Lori was right back where she had started as far as knowing whether Isabel Jessop was telling the truth.

Only after the children had nervously squirmed, until they were excused, did Lori tell them of her experiences at the hotel.

It was Bessie who had brought it up by asking, "Aren't you a little frightened to be out there so far from town?"

"I wasn't until someone tried to scare me by peering in my window wearing a mask."

"A mask! What did it look like?" Anita asked, holding her glass of iced tea in midair.

"It was horrible. Rex told me it was a ceremonial mask like the Indians sometimes wear. Then later that night I saw a strange light near the old ruins. The next day—yesterday—Rex and I went over to take a look around, but it was impossible to tell if anyone had been there. The place was covered with footprints."

Bessie leaned closer. "Do you think it was the same person who wore the mask?"

"It crossed our minds. I saw the light again last night. Earlier in the evening Rex and I were on the patio. One of the guests came out carrying a flashlight. When he saw us, he tried to hide it."

"That sounds suspicious to me," Bessie said, with a nod of approval from Anita. "And it gives me the creeps. Are you sure you want to spend an entire summer out there, Lori?"

"I have to. Besides, I'm not afraid. Rex Fraser is there and I trust him. Anyway, no harm has come to me. Although someone did lock me in the linen closet yesterday."

"Oh, Lori. That sounds serious."

"I was a little panicky. There wasn't that much air in the room. Thank heavens Rex came by when he did and let me out."

Anita was shaking her head. "You should report that to the police, Lori. That is a cruel thing to do to you."

Lori smiled at Bessie's sympathetic sister.

"There really isn't anything I can tell them, Anita. The prowler with the mask never came back. And I don't think there is a law against walking in the desert at night. As for getting myself locked in the closet, they would probably think it was an accident, just as Aunt Hannah feels it was."

"All the same, Lori," Bessie said with a sniff, "you watch yourself out there. It sounds to me as though someone is up to no good. And it looks as if they've got it in for you."

"But why? I haven't done anything to any of the guests. I've never seen them before I arrived at the Crying Winds."

Anita saw how Lori was becoming upset, so she changed the subject. "Tell us about that young man. You said his name was Rex. He sounds like he's looking after you."

Lori felt her face redden as she told the two women about Rex Fraser. She tried not to expose her feelings for the blond giant, but she could tell by the expressions on their faces she wasn't doing a very convincing job.

"You'll have to bring him around sometime," Bessie said. "Before I return to Albuquerque."

"How long will you be staying here?" Lori asked, taking a sip of tea.

"Until Anita and I run out of things to talk about. Or she gets bored with me and asks me to leave."

Anita smiled at her sister. "You know you're free to stay as long as you wish, Bessie. We all love you."

"You mean you love my lemon meringue pie," Bessie replied, and they all laughed.

Lori felt so at home here in the cozy kitchen, she almost dreaded going back to the Crying Winds.

"Speaking of pie, I almost forgot dessert," Anita said as she hurried away to cut generous wedges of the lemon meringue.

Lori was stuffed by the heavy food she had eaten, but the pie did look good and somehow she managed to find room for it.

A half hour later in the small living room, Lori was telling Bessie about the pueblo, since the jovial woman had never been there.

"When we were leaving, I found a pin. It was shaped like a bird and had pieces of turquoise. I have it here in my purse if you care to see it."

When Lori brought out the pin and held it between her fingertips, Anita said, "May I see that a moment, Lori?"

Lori passed the bird over to Anita, who glanced briefly

at it, then said, "Your Aunt Hannah will be glad to get this back. She probably has been looking everywhere for it."

The words that Anita said stunned Lori, so that she could barely say, "This belongs to my aunt?"

Anita nodded as she handed the pin back. "She was very fond of that old bird. Wore it everywhere she went. Like it was a good luck charm or something."

Surely Anita must be mistaken, Lori thought. She remembered how casually Aunt Hannah had looked at the pin and then denied that she had ever seen it.

Suddenly Lori had to leave that house. She had to be alone, to think.

"I'd better be getting back to the Crying Winds," Lori said. "The lunch was wonderful, Anita."

"We must do it again sometime," Bessie's sister said.

After she picked up her perishables, the two women followed Lori to her car and they waved a friendly goodbye as Lori headed back to the hotel.

As she drove through Santa Inez, Lori thought about what Anita had said when she saw the bird. If she had not been mistaken, and the pin was a favorite of Aunt Hannah's, then why had her aunt reacted so indifferently? The mystery of The House of the Crying Winds was deepening, and Lori was becoming more and more confused.

When she got back to the hotel, she hoped that Rex would be there. She had to talk to him about this latest turn of events. She did not think she should just confront her Aunt Hannah with what Anita had said.

For some reason, she was afraid that Hannah Hudson would once again deny ownership of the pin. Yes, she would be glad to see Rex. He was so considerate and dependable, he would know how to handle the situation.

Suddenly Lori wanted a cup of coffee. Bessie's tea had been refreshing, but a cup of coffee was what she needed at the moment. And she was still in the town.

Lori drove as slowly as she dared through the unfamiliar streets of Santa Inez, keeping a wary eye out for a diner or coffee shop. As she neared the outskirts of town, she saw a restaurant on her right and pulled into the parking lot.

Sweeping her purse from the car seat, she locked the door and walked into the restaurant. It was a wide, vast place with tables scattered throughout.

There was a counter near the entrance and Lori perched herself on a stool. All she ordered was a cup of coffee. After the waitress brought it, Lori took a sip and then casually gazed around the room.

At this time of day there was hardly anyone in the room, so she could not help but notice the couple by the far window. A girl with long dark hair was talking animatedly to a blond man who listened intently. Lori's heart seemed to skip a beat. The man sitting with the girl was Rex Fraser.

CHAPTER ELEVEN

Somehow Lori made it out of the restaurant without being seen by Rex. Who was the girl sitting with him? He appeared to be very interested in her. It was as if a huge chunk of ice had been thrust into her stomach. Lori got into her car and drove in the direction of the hotel.

She felt as though she had been spying on Rex and was glad that he hadn't noticed her. How could he? His eyes were all on that beautiful girl with the long dark tresses.

Why shouldn't Rex see another girl? Lori thought, trying to explain his actions to herself. After all, he had never said he was in love with her. Could the girl in the restaurant be someone Rex cared deeply for?

Was Lori just someone to pass the time with during his stay at the Crying Winds? Then, after she had gone back to Ohio, would Rex return to the attractive girl?

"You are jumping at conclusions," Lori said aloud, and the sound of her own voice lifted her sagging spirits.

After all, the girl might just be a good friend of Rex's, nothing more than that. It could have been just a chance meeting and Lori happened to stumble onto them. She had read something into a seemingly harmless situation.

Feeling better, Lori let her thoughts go back to the conversation she had had with Anita about the turquoise bird. It was possible that Bessie's sister might have been mistaken. After all, there were probably many such pins in existence. And if the pin had belonged to Aunt Hannah, she surely would have recognized it and claimed it.

This did not assuage Lori's uncertainties. If the pin was so similar to one her aunt had always worn, then she would have been more curious about it before she so quickly decided it did not belong to her.

After what she had learned at Bessie's sister's house and what she had inadvertently seen at the restaurant, Lori was not overly eager to return to the Crying Winds. She had enjoyed getting away for a few hours, and the prospect of returning to the hotel was a gloomy one.

Even though the Crying Winds was handsomely constructed, there was an atmosphere about the house that disturbed Lori. Now that she was away from the hotel, she could be more objective. Lori could not define what it was, but it was a feeling she could not shake off.

There was something unsettling about the hotel. Her intuition cried out to her. Not only was the hotel unsettling, but there was the threat of danger and bodily harm to her.

Lori shivered despite the warmth from the afternoon sun. She tried to take her mind off such depressing thoughts by looking at the passing scenery. When that did not work, she concentrated on the far purple-hued mountains jutting up against the gorgeous blue sky. A sky that only brought her back to the pin she and Rex had found in the pueblo.

Topping a rise, she could see the hotel below and that gave her mind something to concentrate on. Yet, even as the car moved the last few miles toward the hotel, she thought fleetingly and somewhat despairingly of Rex.

As she neared the hotel, she saw someone walking along the road. It was a woman wearing a floppy hat to ward off the intense rays of the sun. Even from a distance Lori could not fail to recognize the gait of Isabel Jessop. Coming abreast with the woman, Lori braked the car.

"Miss Jessop, would you care for a lift?"

Isabel squinted her eyes until she recognized who the driver of the car was.

"Lori! You are a Samaritan," Isabel said as she opened the door and slipped into the seat. "I don't know what ever possessed me to take such a long walk. You know how I detest the afternoon sun. And any form of exercise is repugnant to me. I always make my walks much shorter."

Isabel removed her floppy hat and proceeded to fan her flushed, florid face. "However, the thought occurred to me today that as long as I was in New Mexico, I should give the sunlight a real try. Ugh! So much for the health routine."

There was a brief silence, then Isabel said, "Incidentally, my dear, what are you doing behind the wheel? Did your aunt give you the day off?"

In the unkind brilliance of the sun Isabel's face took on a hardness Lori had not noticed before.

"There was some shopping to do and Aunt Hannah asked me to go to Santa Inez. I must admit I stayed longer than I should. But I had lunch with some friends and time got away from me."

"I had no idea that you had acquaintances in Santa Inez. You've been here such a brief time."

Lori shifted her attention to the road ahead. "It was someone I met on my trip. A very nice woman and her sister. Frankly, I ate too much."

"At your age that's hardly a monumental problem. It's been years since I can remember eating too much. The camera adds pounds to one's appearance, you know."

With that remark Isabel launched into a long but nevertheless interesting account of a picture she had once made in Paris. As the woman talked, Lori subconsciously wondered how much of what Isabel was saying was the truth. She was still somewhat doubtful as to Isabel's sincerity.

This suspicion had been given reinforcement by the fact that neither Bessie nor Anita had heard of the orange-haired actress, either. Surely someone should have recognized the name of Isabel Jessop.

By the time they reached the entrance to the Crying Winds, Isabel had concluded her vignette.

"So kind of you to give me a lift. Thank you, my dear," Isabel said as she grandly thrust open the door, whipped her Garbolike hat on her head, and hurried away into the depths of the patio.

Although Lori hadn't expected any help with the groceries, she thought it would have been a nice gesture on Isabel's part to have offered to carry even one bag. But, after all, Isabel was a paying guest and Lori shouldn't have anticipated any help.

With a bemused smile, Lori gathered as many bags of groceries as she could, then carried them into the house. When she finished putting the food away, Lori spent an hour dusting and vacuuming the living and dining rooms. This kept her mind off Rex and what Anita had told her earlier that day.

As she was putting the vacuum cleaner away in the hall, Nancy Neeley wandered into the living room. She had not seen Lori and she looked around quickly and then went to the registration desk. Mrs. Neeley began looking around the desk with a consuming interest. Lori felt she should make her presence known before it became an embarrassment to both herself and the woman.

Lori slammed the door with a deliberate motion. Then she pretended that she had just seen Nancy Neeley, who stood rigidly at the registration desk.

"Hello, Mrs. Neeley. Is there anything I can help you with?"

Nancy Neeley quickly recovered her icy composure and

with a tilt of her chin said, "I was just checking to see if the mail had arrived."

"It's on the end of the desk," Lori said, advancing toward the woman. "Where it's always kept."

Nancy's cool eyes swept over Lori before she said, "Your aunt sometimes delivers the mail."

"That's true. However, she has been very busy today. I've been away shopping for the hotel and my aunt just didn't have time."

"I see," Nancy replied, and she picked up the stack of mail and went quickly through the letters. Apparently, there was nothing for the Neeleys, so she replaced the letters with a distracted air.

"We travel so much, our mail has a difficult time in keeping up with us."

"That can be a problem," Lori said.

Nancy shrugged. "Nothing insurmountable. Are you enjoying your stay in New Mexico?"

Lori was surprised at Nancy's tone of voice. It was almost pleasant. "Very much. I wish my parents could be here to enjoy it also."

Nancy raised an inquisitive eyebrow. "Where are your parents? Back in Ohio?"

Lori shook her head. "In Europe. Dad promised Mother he would take her there when he retired. So he's making good his promise."

"Then there is no one who would miss you back in Ohio?"

Lori thought that was an odd question and the way Nancy had said it was even odder.

"You might say that. However, I do have my aunt, so I am near a relative. Even though this is the first time I have ever met Aunt Hannah."

"What is your opinion of your aunt?"

The question was so sudden, it almost caught Lori off-guard.

"She's a difficult person to get to know. But I can understand that. Aunt Hannah has always been an independent person. Or so my father has told me. I feel sure that by the time summer is over, we will have become fast friends."

Nancy Neeley said, "This is hardly the place for a girl of your age. I can't help but wonder why you came in the first place."

Gone was the warmth that Lori had detected in Nancy earlier. Mrs. Neeley had retreated back into her aloof, cynical shell.

"Aunt Hannah asked me to come. She needed help. Apparently, she was having difficulty in getting anyone to work this far from Santa Inez."

"That is very commendable of you, or very foolish."

Lori glared at the disagreeable woman.

"Foolish! In what way?"

"Anything could happen to you this far out in the desert. Or hadn't you thought about that?"

"An accident could happen to me at home as easily as here," Lori retorted.

"That wasn't what I had in mind," came the cool response.

"Just what did you have in mind?"

Nancy Neeley had suddenly lost interest in the conversation. With a shrug of her shoulders, she turned and ambled toward the door. Before she stepped outside, she turned to Lori and said cryptically, "If I were you, I would be very careful while I was here this summer."

The door slammed behind Nancy while Lori gazed after her in bewilderment. Was Nancy referring to the "accidents" that had happened to Lori since she arrived at the Crying Winds? There was little doubt in Lori's mind that

Nancy Neeley was as suspicious a person as her husband.

Could it have been Nancy who had watched her yesterday until she was alone in the closet? She could have quietly slipped into the hall and shut the closet door.

I wouldn't put it past her, Lori said to herself as she pivoted and walked purposefully toward her room to fix her hair and clean up.

Moments later, Lori headed for the kitchen. As she passed her aunt's room, she saw that the door was open. Cautiously Lori rapped on the open door.

"Aunt Hannah? Are you there? It's me, Lori."

Since there was no answer, Lori assumed her aunt was still busy working somewhere in the hotel. Reaching out for the doorknob, Lori found her gaze resting on the dressing table that stood against the far wall. What she saw caused her to pause.

Arranged in a neat row were five wooden heads, each wearing a different wig, and each wig was a different shade. It was so surprising that Lori could not believe what she was seeing. The wigs must have been quite expensive because they looked so lifelike.

Lori suddenly felt as though she were prying into her aunt's personal life. She quickly closed the door. Not any too soon, for Aunt Hannah chose to come down the hall at that moment.

"You're back. Did you have any trouble with my order?"

Lori quickly recovered from what she had seen in her aunt's room. "Not the least. I could have been back earlier, but I had lunch with some friends in town. I hope you don't mind."

Aunt Hannah snorted. "Why should I mind? I didn't think you knew anybody in New Mexico."

"It was a woman I met on the bus. Her name's Bessie. She invited me to lunch and I accepted. I got back about an hour ago and I cleaned up the living room."

"It could use it. I think I'll clean up a bit before supper. Thanks for shopping for me, Lori."

Aunt Hannah entered her room and quickly closed the door behind her. For a moment Lori stood there pondering in her mind the array of wigs in her aunt's room. When a person wore Levi's and flannel shirts for her daily garb, it was surprising to find expensive wigs in her room. Lori felt she would never understand her aunt, no matter how long she stayed at the Crying Winds.

Dinner was a hastily prepared meal of baked lamb chops and rice. Without Oscar T. Owens present, Isabel Jessop had very little competition for the center of attention.

Rex came in late and he took a seat next to Lori. If there had been anything between himself and the girl in the restaurant, he did not betray his feelings in any manner.

He chatted amiably with Lori and she found herself swept away by the blond giant's charm. Within a few minutes, she had completely forgotten the girl she had seen him with earlier that day.

The Neeleys were the same distant people. They listened politely but somewhat smugly as Isabel did her best to beguile everyone with her nonstop chatter. Aunt Hannah paid little, if any, attention to what went on around her. She ate ravenously. Lori was amazed at her aunt's capacity for food. But then she did work hard all day and that would account for her healthy appetite.

At one point Isabel drew a breath, then said, "We are missing one person. Where is dear Mr. Owens?"

Aunt Hannah took a sip of coffee before saying, "He had some work in town. Won't be back until later."

"Pity," Isabel said, very unconvincingly, before she continued her verbal marathon.

Lori was glad when the meal was over. Isabel was beginning to get on her nerves. The Neeleys must have

felt the same way, for they excused themselves and returned to their room soon after they had finished eating.

Undaunted by the lack of a big audience, Isabel cornered
Rex and Hannah Hudson as she maneuvered them into the
living room. Lori took the supper dishes into the kitchen,
grateful to have some free time to herself. When she had
finished washing the dishes, Rex strolled in.

"A bit of Isabel goes a long, long way," he said, and
Lori laughed. "You don't mind if I take refuge here for
a few minutes, do you?"

"Be my guest," replied Lori, putting the last dish away
in the cupboard.

"So you went to Santa Inez today. Hannah told me she
gave you some free time. Did you have a good trip?"

Lori nodded. "I'm afraid the scenery of New Mexico
is beginning to get to me. I'll miss it when I go back to
Ohio. How was your day?"

Rex shrugged his massive shoulders. "I was out in the
wilderness all day, shooting some film. Didn't see a living
soul."

Lori tried not to stare at him, afraid that her face would
betray her disbelief. Rex had lied to her. He did not want
to tell her about being in Santa Inez—and with the beautiful
dark-haired girl.

CHAPTER TWELVE

For the rest of the evening, Lori found herself having mixed feelings toward Rex. He had lied to her concerning his whereabouts that day and she felt as though she had been betrayed.

There were so many things she wanted to talk over with him. There was the matter of the turquoise pin and what Bessie's sister had said about it. Why would Aunt Hannah deny it belonged to her? There were also the wigs she had seen in her aunt's room.

Lori's father often spoke of his eccentric sister. One of the qualities Lori remembered was her total lack of interest in her personal appearance. Hannah Hudson, according to her brother, cared very little for style or any frills at all.

If this had once been true, then Hannah had changed greatly since her brother had seen her. The wigs in her room attested to that.

Now, as the four people sat in the living room sipping coffee, Lori occasionally glanced at her aunt as though she were seeing her for the first time.

"You seem lost in your thoughts," Rex said, and Lori was jarred back to the immediate moment.

"I'm sorry. I wasn't listening."

"That's obvious," Rex said. "Isabel was asking you about your trip to Santa Inez."

"I thought we talked about that earlier," Lori said somewhat irritably.

"It wasn't important," came Isabel's voice, although the implication was that any question she asked demanded an answer.

The atmosphere suddenly changed as the front door banged open and shut and Oscar T. Owens came barging into the living room.

"This looks like a cozy gathering. Have I had a day! I'm hungry as a bear. There wouldn't be any scraps left over from dinner by any chance?"

Before Lori could answer, Aunt Hannah sprang from her chair. Lori noticed how her aunt always became more alive and animated when the pudgy man was around.

"You take a seat, Mr. Owens, and I'll rustle up something for you. Don't get up, Lori. You stay with the others. It won't take me a minute."

Aunt Hannah scurried out of the room. Her movements were those of a woman many years younger than the age of Hannah Hudson.

Oh, well, Lori thought, so she likes Oscar T. Owens. What harm is there in that? It was just that Lori could not picture herself ever, in the future, calling the corpulent man Uncle Oscar. Lori inwardly winced at that idea.

"How was your day, Isabel, old girl," Oscar said to the actress, who stiffened at the familiarity of the remark.

"Bucolic. I took a long walk away from the hotel. I was saved from sunstroke only by the mercy of Lori. There might be a lot to say for the sun, but it's wasted on me. Frankly, I'm a night person."

This remark garnered Lori's attention.

"A night person? By that I gather you're often up rather late."

"Merely a rebellion against all those early morning studio calls. Although I loved them, don't get me wrong.

Now that I am temporarily between films, I enjoy staying up late. Besides, I suffer from insomnia."

So Isabel was awake and about late at night. Could she have been the person Lori had seen with the light? Even though Isabel gave the impression that she was quite helpless, she could very easily be pretending.

If Isabel was the person Lori had seen, what was she doing going to the ruins? Even if Isabel was more robust than she appeared, it was still impossible to imagine her using a shovel in the dead of night while she searched for buried treasure. Unless she had an accomplice. Or maybe she hadn't been at the pueblo in search of the turquoise. Lori could very easily be off the track entirely.

Aunt Hannah returned with a tray of food for Oscar, and she all but tucked his napkin under his chin for him.

'Thank you, Hannah," Oscar said offhandedly as he continued to talk to the others.

It embarrassed Lori the way the man treated her aunt. And what was worse, Aunt Hannah appeared to dote on Oscar.

At around eleven o'clock, Isabel left to be followed shortly by Oscar. Aunt Hannah took the tray into the kitchen, leaving Lori and Rex alone. But Lori felt ill at ease around the blond giant.

"Is there anything bothering you?" Rex asked after Aunt Hannah had gone.

"Nothing," Lori said hastily. She could not look Rex in the eye for fear of giving herself away. "Why do you ask?"

"I don't know. Somehow I got the feeling that you had something on your mind. Something that was making you withdrawn."

Lori evaded the arm Rex tried to put around her shoulders.

"I'll have to be honest. That's the way I am. When I

was leaving Santa Inez today, I stopped for a cup of coffee in some restaurant I saw along the way. When I came inside, you were there at a table by the window. And you were not alone."

Lori had been watching Rex's face, and his reaction was almost one of anger. "That's right. I was with a girl. Her name is Sharon. And I can't tell you any more about her at this time."

"You can't, or you won't?" Lori snapped.

"Have it your way. I can see that you are not in the mood to be reasonable."

"What can you expect when you deliberately lied to me?"

Rex's frown deepened. "I had my reasons for saying what I did. All I can ask is that you trust me."

"I'm afraid I cannot do that. How do I know that what you've told me in the past is the truth?"

"Then I guess there isn't anything more to be said," Rex replied as he walked purposefully toward the door.

When the door slammed behind Rex, it was as though her heart had been stepped on. Lori turned out the lights in the living room and made certain the front door was bolted.

As she walked to her bedroom, she found that she had clenched her fists until her knuckles ached. All she could think was, Why, why, why? Why had Rex lied to her? And when she had confronted him, he more or less told her it was none of her business.

By the time she got to her room, there were tears in her eyes. Tears of anger mingled with a sharp pain of hurt. She had fallen in love with Rex Fraser, and she had made a fool of herself.

That part hurt more than the fact that she had given her heart to him. It was obvious now that Rex was insincere in his affection toward her. All she was was a summer diversion, someone he would forget the minute she boarded the plane back to Ohio.

"I'll go back home," Lori said aloud.

But the words had a hollow ring to them. Going back home would be admitting defeat, admitting she was incapable of acting on her own without the help of her parents. She couldn't run out on her aunt, although she was not certain that Hannah Hudson would be all that saddened if she did decide to leave. No, she would stay, even though it would be difficult seeing Rex Fraser every day.

After she had slipped into bed, she lay there staring at the gray ceiling, trying desperately to fall asleep. Her mind would not allow this to happen. It raced anxiously over the events of the day.

Lori thought about the wigs, the talk with Bessie and her sister, the painful moment when she accidentally saw Rex and Sharon in the restaurant. In order not to think of Rex and the reality of his lying to her, she let her mind dwell on Aunt Hannah.

Anita had been so certain that the turquoise pin belonged to Aunt Hannah. If this were true, then why had her aunt denied ownership? Could the answer be that—that the woman here at the hotel was not the real Hannah Hudson?

Lori sat up in bed. The moon's bright light bathed the room in a luminous glow. She found that she was shivering. And she knew that it was not because she was cold.

What had ever possessed her to think such a terrible thing of her aunt? To think that she was an imposter? Lori flung away the covers and got out of bed. She draped a robe about her shoulders as she walked restlessly toward the patio.

Once outside the sliding glass doors, Lori took deep breaths of the fresh air. The wind was crying mournfully through the branches of the trees, and the sound was a haunting background to her dismal thoughts. It must have

been the shock of seeing Rex with another woman that
had caused her to think such thoughts of Aunt Hannah.

After all, the woman did invite Lori to come for the
summer and at times she was almost civil to her. Was it
merely the fact that Hannah Hudson was so aloof and
difficult to get to know that had caused Lori's imagination
to run away with itself? That had to be the answer.

Glancing out across the wide expanse of land, Lori was
not surprised when she saw the light once again. She stood
on the patio watching until the flickering glow vanished
among the remains of the pueblo. This was another mystery which she wanted desperately to find the solution to.
But then she yawned, feeling a welcome drowsiness flow
over her.

Lori went back to bed and slept soundly. Her dreams
were of Rex and in them he appeared to be always re-
moving a mask from his face, revealing another crafty,
unpleasant visage beneath the mask.

She awoke suddenly and found the bed covers were
entangled around her body. Disentangling the covers, she
once again got out of bed. The lamb chops she had eaten
at supper had made her thirsty. She thought about going
to the kitchen and fixing herself a glass of milk.

By this time, Lori had become accustomed to the house
and she moved through the living room without turning
on a light. Besides, the glare might awaken Aunt Hannah.

Walking into the kitchen, Lori flicked on the light and
got a carton of milk from the refrigerator. Taking it to the
countertop near the sink, she paused when she saw a plate
which still had the remnants of food on it.

She had thought Aunt Hannah had washed up after
Oscar had finished his supper. But as she looked closer,
she saw that this was a different plate than the one her aunt
had used to serve Mr. Owens.

Most of the plates that were used for serving food had

a thunderbird design on them. This plate was one Lori had never seen before.

After Lori had poured herself a glass of milk, she sat at the kitchen table. From where she sat she could see the plate on the countertop. She felt certain that nobody had come into the kitchen after she had gone to bed, since she had bolted the door separating this section of the house from the guest rooms. Then how could she explain the plate, and who had been secretly eating in the kitchen? Aunt Hannah? That seemed unlikely. This mystery gave Lori an eerie feeling, so she quickly drank her milk and hurried back to her room.

Oscar T. Owens had explained away the missing portion of the roast, but who would come up with an explanation for the late-night snack in the kitchen? Lori crawled into bed and fluffed the pillows. She was suddenly too tired to let her mind dwell on what she had found in the kitchen. She yawned widely, then drifted off to a dream-free sleep.

For the next few days Lori stayed as busy as she could, and the time went quickly. She made a point of not sitting next to Rex at any of the meals, and she was polite yet distant to him, answering his questions but never volunteering any conversation on her own part.

Rex at first appeared hurt by her actions. Then, as the days went by, he seemed to accept her avoidance with a cool indifference. Lori at times regretted her actions, but she could not help herself. It was almost impossible for her to forget that Rex had lied to her.

Aunt Hannah had given her Tuesdays off, and on her first free Tuesday she just did some shopping in Santa Inez. But on her second free Tuesday she borrowed her aunt's Volkswagen, packed a picnic lunch, and went for a drive. The land around the Crying Winds, she discovered, had many roads. Some were in good condition, while others were merely pathways.

As she drove, the warm wind tousled her tawny hair, and she felt free and adventuresome. It was only when she stopped to eat that she realized it would have been so much more fun to share her lunch with someone. And she knew who that someone was. Rex Fraser.

Lately Rex had been less distant toward her, almost as though he were apologetic for not having told her the truth about the girl in Santa Inez. Lori missed their talks and his closeness at the dining-room table. She needed someone she could confide in.

Maybe she should never have brought up the incident of the restaurant. After all, it could have been a perfectly harmless meeting and she could have jumped to conclusions.

She made up her mind as she munched on a chicken leg that when she returned to the hotel she would be more civil toward Rex. In time, perhaps, the whole unpleasant scene would be forgotten.

Now that she had made up her mind, Lori felt better than she had for days. She gazed around at her surroundings and glanced upward at the turquoise blue sky. She doubted that she would ever grow tired of that endless stretch of blue or the rugged, stark landscape. She would have to ask Rex for some photographs to send to her parents so that they could share the beauty of this awesome land.

Thinking about her parents, she hoped they were having a good time in Europe. She was suddenly very happy that they had had the good sense not to take her along. What an exchange of impressions and adventures they could share when summer was ended and she returned to Ohio.

Lori walked up a small nearby hill after she finished eating. Below her stretched the valley with The House of the Crying Winds standing starkly in the afternoon sunlight.

From this distance it appeared so tranquil, not giving a hint of the mysteries that came with nightfall.

Having her fill of the view, Lori returned to her car and headed back to the hotel. She drove hastily, for she was anxious to get back to the Crying Winds. She wanted to see Rex to try and make amends for her behavior.

It was still early in the afternoon, and there was still plenty of time left of her day off. Maybe Rex might even ask to take her to Santa Inez to a movie or a restaurant.

Arriving at the hotel, Lori parked the car in the garage, then hurried across the patio. As she was passing the wrought-iron gate, she saw a car drive slowly past the hotel. The vehicle was going at such a slow rate of speed that she could easily see who the driver was. Her heart sank. The driver of the car was Sharon.

CHAPTER THIRTEEN

After Sharon's car had moved away, Lori stood for a moment or two without moving. It would be impossible now to talk to Rex. All the thoughts she had earlier that afternoon suddenly were gone from her mind.

Sharon knew where Rex was staying, and it was obvious that she was looking for him. Just how much did Sharon mean to Rex? From the little Lori had seen of the woman, she knew that it would be impossible to compete with Sharon. If ever there was someone with beauty-contest winner stamped all over her, the girl with the long, dark hair was it.

Lori walked wearily toward the part of the hotel where she and her aunt shared their quarters.

"Lori, how furtunate to find you," came the familiar voice of Isabel Jessop, who came walking briskly up the walk. "I'm simply perishing from thirst. Would it be too much to ask for a glass of iced tea?"

"Of course not," Lori replied, grateful to the actress for temporarily faking her mind off her problems.

"I haven't seen you since breakfast. Have you been to Santa Inez again?"

"This is my day off. I went for a ride in the hills."

Isabel lifted her outsized sunglasses to the crown of her head. "How nice. For you, of course, but not for me. Did you have a companion on the drive? By that I mean a certain Mr. Rex Fraser."

Lori felt her face flame at the mention of Rex's name. "I was alone. As far as Rex Fraser is concerned, I have no idea how he spent the day."

"I see," the actress said as her watery eyes narrowed. "Of course it's none of my business, but did you two have a spat?"

"You're right, Miss Jessop, it is none of your business," Lori replied sharply, then regretted her remark. "I'm sorry. I didn't mean to snap at you."

Isabel shrugged elaborately. "Think nothing of it. In the world of the theater, one must develop a thick hide. Or one won't survive."

Inside the house Lori and Isabel went to the kitchen where Lori poured them some iced tea in frosted glasses. She found some cookies which she put on a small plate and the two of them sat at the small kitchen table.

Isabel took a sip of the tea before she spoke. "That was refreshing. Now tell me what's troubling you?"

"I don't know what you mean," Lori said, avoiding Isabel Jessop's eyes.

"Don't you? It's been fairly obvious to everyone the way you've been avoiding Rex Fraser. I thought you were good friends."

"We were," Lori said defensively. "Only, I thought we were becoming too serious. After all, I know nothing about Mr. Fraser. And I am only staying for the duration of the summer."

"What has that got to do with anything?" Isabel remarked after she had nibbled on a cookie. "Rex is a very charming man. He would make a good companion for you. I certainly find him most attractive."

It was obvious from the fading actress's voice that she did find Rex attractive. Lori wondered just how much.

She was tempted to tell Isabel about Sharon but thought better of it.

Somehow she still did not entirely trust Isabel Jessop. Although the woman was far more open and likable than either her aunt or Nancy Neeley. It bothered Lori to think such thoughts of her aunt, although she had no reason to feel otherwise.

"I agree with you, Rex is quite an attractive person. However, he has his work as do I. Besides, when his assignment is ended, he'll be on his way."

"And you don't relish the thought of being left high and dry. Is that it, my pet?"

Isabel had said these words with such sarcasm that Lori was too startled to make a rebuttal.

"Like I said before, you should leave this place, Lori. Before it's too late."

With that Isabel got to her feet. "Thank you for the tea. It was quite refreshing."

After the actress had gone, Lori sat at the table staring at the melting ice cubes in her glass. Another warning to leave the Crying Winds. Isabel was the most changeable person she had ever encountered in her life. Lori wondered if Isabel meant what she said about her leaving the hotel. With Isabel it was almost impossible to tell whether she was acting or not.

"Forget it," Lori said aloud and went to rinse out the glasses.

Even though it was her day off, she glazed a ham and put it in the oven to bake. Aunt Hannah had her hands full with the guest quarters. Fixing supper would at least take that burden off her hands.

When she had finished, Lori strolled out of the kitchen to her room. As she was passing through the living room, the telephone rang. Quickening her stride, Lori caught the phone on its third ring.

"House of the Crying Winds," she said, realizing it was the first time she had answered the phone that way.

There was a brief pause at the other end of the line. Then a woman asked to speak to Rex Fraser. Since there were no telephones as yet installed in the rooms, Lori told the woman she would see if Rex was in his room.

Lori hurried to Rex's room, all the time wondering who the woman was. Since she had never heard Sharon's voice, she could not be certain that was who was on the phone. She rapped on the door, lightly at first, and then more loudly.

"Rex?" she called out. "There is a phone call for you."

She paused and waited. There was no sign that Rex was in his room. Lori wondered why she felt relieved that he wasn't there.

Assured that he was not available, Lori rushed back to the living room.

"I'm sorry, Mr. Fraser is out at the moment. May I have him return the call?"

Again there was a brief, hesitant pause on the other end of the line. Then the voice said, "No, thank you. I'll try again later."

There was a click as the woman hung up. Lori replaced the receiver in its cradle with deep concern. There was little doubt in her mind now that the caller had been Sharon. She entertained the idea of putting a note on Rex's door saying he had received a phone call from a woman, then dismissed the thought. Sharon said she would call back and maybe, if Lori were lucky, she wouldn't be around when the call came through.

Lori couldn't understand her emotions. She was torn between feelings of hurt and jealousy. Ever since she met Rex, he had appeared so sincere and acted as though he really cared for her. Yet all the while he and Sharon had had something going.

It would be better for Lori if she continued to keep a distance between herself and Rex. Otherwise, she knew she could be terribly hurt by Rex Fraser.

With a regretful sigh, Lori went to her room and took a shower. She felt somewhat better as the stinging water bounced off her body. She selected a green linen dress and brushed her hair until it glistened with a lustrous sheen.

Lori knew that secretly she was doing her best to compete with the beauteous Sharon. When she looked in the mirror, she was satisfied that she could give the brunette a run for her money.

Fastening a strand of imitation pearls about her throat, she tossed her head, then walked from the room with more self-confidence than she had felt in days.

Aunt Hannah was emerging from her room, apparently unaware of Lori's presence. Lori paused as she saw her aunt tug at a strand of copper-colored hair, which she eased quickly beneath her iron-gray hairdo.

Now Lori's suspicions were confirmed. Hannah Hudson was wearing a wig. But why would she want to disguise such obviously pretty hair? If Lori hadn't seen the wigs in her aunt's room, this gesture on her part would have come as a startling surprise.

Hannah Hudson turned and saw Lori for the first time. For once the chilly composure of her aunt was gone. "Lori! How long have you been standing there?"

"Just a moment," Lori muttered, not quite knowing what to say to her aunt.

"I was in the kitchen earlier and caught a whiff of the ham," Aunt Hannah said. "So I gathered you were back. Where did you go on your day off?"

Lori moved tentatively, somewhat awkwardly, across the hall. "Oh, I just drove around. No place in particular. I hope you weren't too busy while I was away."

Aunt Hannah had regained her regal composure. "Busy

enough. I'd better get the table set up for supper. This being your day off, you can relax."

"If you don't mind, I'll finish up what I started in the kitchen. In a way I want to stay busy."

Aunt Hannah shrugged. "Suit yourself."

Lori couldn't help noticing the way her aunt looked at her with her emerald green eyes before she entered the dining room. It could have been the dim lighting, but Lori felt that her aunt was looking at her with anger and suspicion.

Somehow she managed to get the food on the table. Rex was late arriving and it took every bit of control Lori could muster to treat him civilly.

"You must have a trunkful of pictures by this time, Rex," Oscar T. Owens said, helping himself to a thick slice of ham.

Rex sipped some water as he stared at the obese man. "My assignment is coming along very well. I hope to wind up my job before too long."

At these words Lori felt a pang of hurt in the pit of her stomach. So Rex would be leaving before long. Oh, well, she had known that someday she would have to face up to that fact.

After supper Isabel told them she would give a performance. This was met with mixed feelings by those assembled. For Lori it was exciting. She wanted to see whether Isabel could live up to the legend she had been creating among those living at the Crying Winds.

Rex sat next to her on the couch, but Lori tried to keep some distance between them. She chatted with the other guests in a nervous fashion until her aunt fixed a frosty glare upon her.

Isabel took the center of attention as she began her performance. At first the aging actress appeared to be slightly nervous and her voice wavered somewhat. Then, as she threw herself into her role, she changed before Lori's eyes.

This was a different person from the flamboyant woman who postured around the hotel. Isabel actually became the character she was portraying. When she finished, everyone in the room applauded vigorously.

"You were wonderful, Isabel," Lori said as she went to congratulate the woman. "You're a wonderful actress."

"Was there any doubt?" Isabel replied, once again slipping into the familiar role she played offstage.

Even the Neeleys were impressed. They looked at Isabel with new respect.

Oscar T. Owens was the only fly in the ointment when he said, "Don't get me wrong, old girl, I enjoyed it. Even though I enjoy a good prizefight more than anything else."

Isabel ignored the rude, dumpy man and he wandered over to speak to Hannah Hudson. Whatever he said to Aunt Hannah made her look nervously around and Lori saw her aunt get to her feet and hurry out of the room to the kitchen. After that Lori poured coffee for everyone and she forgot all about her aunt.

As they were sipping their coffee, the telephone jangled. Lori glanced around to see if Aunt Hannah was anywhere in sight. She dreaded answering the phone because of her experience earlier that day.

Finally it became apparent that she couldn't ignore the persistent ringing, and she hurried to the desk where she picked up the receiver. It was for Rex, a woman calling, and Lori knew that it must be Sharon.

She tried to focus her attention on the rest of the guests, but her thoughts were on Rex and his phone call. He spoke too softly for Lori to make out his words, and when he hung up, his face was inscrutable.

Somehow the evening came to an end. Rex was the last person to leave.

"Lori, why are you doing this?" he asked abruptly.

"Doing what?"

"Ignoring me. It's been pretty obvious."

"You should know the answer to that."

Rex's face became granite hard.

"It's not what you are thinking. I'd like us to be friends."

"We are friends."

The hard lines in his face softened. "Good. Maybe on your next free day, you might consider going with me to Albuquerque."

Lori couldn't face his direct, unwavering stare. "I'll think about it."

"I couldn't ask for more than that. Good night."

With that Rex walked out of the living-room door, leaving Lori alone in the big room. Moments later she walked with weary steps to her room. Rex could be so charming when he wanted to be.

But what lurked behind that charm? She knew the phone call had been from Sharon, yet he had said nothing about it. Lori was confused and dejected.

She did not feel like going to bed. Her mind was racing a mile a minute. Instead, she picked up a book she had purchased in Santa Inez and curled up in bed near the lamp to read it.

The book was a modern novel and Lori found it could not hold her interest. Partly because she could not identify with the dim-witted heroine too strongly. When she found that she had read one paragraph three times, and still could not remember what she had read, she put the book aside and eased herself off the bed. She was restless and not the least bit sleepy.

The house sighed with the crying winds, sounding so mournful that Lori shuddered involuntarily. To take her mind off the sound, she thought about Aunt Hannah and the wig she wore. Now, more than ever, Lori was hesitant

to confront her aunt again with the turquoise pin. There
was something very strange going on here at the hotel.
Even though the "accidents" and "practical jokes" had
ceased, she still had an uneasy feeling that things were not
right here.

Suddenly the room was suffocating and airless. Lori
walked over to the patio doors and flung them open. At
once the cool night breeze rushed in upon her. She took
in several deep breaths, then stepped onto the shadowy
patio.

Overhead the sky was aglow with brilliant stars. Yet
Lori could not appreciate the beauty. She was still thinking
of Rex when she saw the light in the distance. It wavered
as it moved through the darkness. Lori could no longer
bear not to know who was walking toward the deserted
pueblo.

Impulsively she pivoted and scurried back into the
room. She grabbed a sweater from the closet and hastily
slipped her arms into the sleeves. Then she hurried into
the living room and picked up a flashlight she had discovered during one of her cleaning forays.

Cautiously, she opened the front door and closed it
softly so as not to disturb Aunt Hannah or anyone else.
Once outside, Lori hurried in the direction she had seen
the mysterious light.

CHAPTER FOURTEEN

Passing through the patio Lori toyed with the idea of waking Rex and telling him what she was planning to do. Then she decided not to. At one time she wouldn't have hesitated in calling on him for assistance. All that was changed now.

"Anyway, I'll be careful and not do anything foolish," she muttered to herself as she crossed the patio and opened the wrought-iron gate.

Crossing the road she found herself in open country and she flicked on the flashlight. Its yellow beam cut through the darkness like a sharp knife. She took cautious steps, feeling the grainy, sandy soil beneath her shoes.

When she had gone some distance, she paused by a clump of bushes and let her eyes scan the area where she had seen the wavering light. The glare from her flashlight made it difficult to see, so she switched off the light. Lori stood for a moment until her eyes became accustomed to the darkness.

Ahead of her and to her right she saw the faint glimmer of a light. It moved spectral-like in the shrouded darkness. Standing alone with the wind whispering through the underbrush she felt a chill go down her spine, and she fleetingly thought of returning to the safety of her room.

"You've come this far, you can't go back now," she said aloud, hoping those words would bolster her courage.

As she started to continue, something moved in a thicket in front of her. Frightened, Lori turned on the flashlight and moved it in the direction of the noise. Two eyes glistened for an instant, caught in the paralyzing glare. Then a jackrabbit bounded away into the surrounding darkness. With a sigh of relief, Lori once more began picking her way toward the pueblo.

She wondered who she might find there and, more important, what the person was doing in the ruins so late at night. Was she coming closer to solving the enigma of The House of the Crying Winds?

With each step she felt she was coming closer to the answer to a lot of questions. Who had worn the ceremonial mask to frighten her that first night? Was it the same person who had locked her in the linen closet?

In her mind's eye, Lori saw the faces of the lodgers who were staying at the hotel. Could the person ahead of her be one of them? Isabel Jessop claimed she had insomnia and could not rest at night. Was this a coverup for her wandering at night in case someone discovered that she was not in her room?

Even though Isabel had proven she possessed talent tonight, there was still something about the woman that suggested she was not telling the whole truth about herself.

As for Oscar T. Owens, he was such a loud, blustering person, it was hard for Lori to imagine him being anything other than what he was. A salesman. Still, his being a salesman could just be a front. He could easily have heard the legend of the missing turquoise and have come here in search of it.

She did not like the way he exercised so much control over her aunt. Whatever attracted Aunt Hannah to the corpulent man was beyond Lori.

A vagrant cloud had passed over the moon, temporarily bathing the land in darkness. This made it easier for Lori to detect the faint glimmer of light in the distance. She had come quite a way from the hotel and she turned back to see its faint outline as the moon emerged from behind the cloud.

Back there, Rex was probably sleeping away. Dreaming of Sharon, Lori thought bitterly as she blinked back tears of hurt and frustration. She could not help herself. Even though Rex had deliberately lied to her, she still loved him. He was the most handsome, exciting man she had ever met in her life.

Why had she allowed herself to be attracted to the man when she knew he would be leaving before the end of the summer? It hadn't been planned, it had just happened. Sometimes she wished she had never gone into that restaurant that day in Santa Inez. If she hadn't seen Rex with Sharon, she would never have been the wiser, and she wouldn't be going through all this heartache.

Turning from the sight of the hotel, Lori continued following the light that by now had grown dimmer. She quickened her stride, once nearly tripping over a dark rock which she mistook for a shadow.

"Watch where you're going," she chided herself. "If you twist your ankle, you'll be in a fine mess!"

Hearing her own voice boosted her sagging confidence and she picked her way carefully through her unfamiliar surroundings.

The ruins loomed ahead now, jagged, serrated bits of adobe that wind and rain were slowly reducing to rubble. She was glad that Rex had taken her to see the pueblo. At least that gave her some idea of what to expect when she actually arrived at the ruins.

Now that she was approaching the pueblo she saw that the light had vanished. For the first time Lori began to realize the folly of what she had done. Nobody knew that she was out here.

Perhaps it would have been wiser to have asked Rex to come along. Or maybe she should have left a note telling Aunt Hannah where she had gone. Lori knew that would have been a mistake. Aunt Hannah would be furious with her if she knew Lori was out prowling around the ruins so late at night.

When she was about twenty feet from the entrance to the pueblo, Lori came to an abrupt halt. She switched off her light and listened for any sound coming from within the pueblo.

At first there was nothing but the ever-present wind. Then she thought she heard a scraping sound, followed by a hollow thud. The noise sounded like a heavy object being dropped in place. Whoever was in the pueblo was looking for something. Lori moved cautiously toward the ruins.

Inside the decaying doorways and the crumbling interiors were dark shadows. Lori looked around, but there was no sign of anyone else in the pueblo. Fearful that whoever was there might have seen her, she kept to the shadows exposing as little of herself as possible.

The pueblo was so different by moonlight. It had been awesome during the daylight hours and she had not been particularly frightened. Then Rex had been with her, she remembered. Now each gust of wind and each black shadow held a threat of danger. Lori wondered who might be lurking in the black depths beyond the doorways.

Once she thought she saw something move at the far end of the ruins. She caught her breath and hugged an adobe wall with her back, all the while not taking her eyes from the place where she had seen the movement. After a while, when her back began to ache from the stiffness she had imposed upon it, she decided it had just been her imagination.

Stepping away from the wall, Lori walked toward the

kiva, which housed the underground rooms the Indians used during some of their ceremonies. She had decided that this would be the last place she would look. Then, after that, she would go back to the hotel.

Moving toward the kiva she suddenly heard a noise from one of the deserted rooms to her right. Turning on her flashlight, Lori moved in that direction. A blast of wind carrying a spray of fine sand was flung into her face and temporarily blinded her. Rubbing the grit from her eyes with the sleeve of her sweater, Lori walked toward a darkened archway.

"Is there anyone there?" she cried out as her light moved into the depths of the archway. The only answer was the mournful lamentation of the wind. Yet Lori felt someone was inside the dark room.

Tentatively she took a step forward, and the beam from her flashlight danced across the darkness. Then she heard the movement of something inside the room. Fingers reached out and grabbed the flashlight from her hand. Lori shrieked and swirled around. Her only thought was to get away from this terrorizing place.

She began to run, unmindful of the direction she was going. Behind her she thought she heard the sound of pursuing footsteps. She dared not look around to see who it might be. Her heart was pounding fiercely and she was gasping for air.

Ahead of her she saw the open stretch of country. If only she could make it she felt she would be free of her pursuer.

Lori was running in such a state of panic that she did not see the rock which jutted up from the ground. Her foot struck the rock and she fell down helplessly. She struggled desperately to get to her feet, then felt the force of something striking her head before she was pitched into oblivion.

When Lori opened her eyes, she was lying on her back. Above her the stars still glistened in the night sky. For a moment she could not remember where she was or how she happened to be lying on the sand.

She shifted her gaze and saw a figure looming above her. Lori gasped.

"Are you all right?" came a man's voice. "You've been out for some time."

The figure moved closer and in the moonlight Lori recognized the face of Ray Neeley.

"I think I'm all right. There was a rock. I remember tripping over it."

Ray Neeley reached down and took her hands, helping her to her feet. She found her legs were somewhat wobbly.

"How did you happen to be out here at this time of night?" Ray asked.

Lori wasn't certain she could trust the man. After all, it could very easily have been he who had struck her on the head.

"1 was restless and thought I would take a walk. I never intended to go this far," she said.

Ray appeared to be thinking over what she had said. "It's very dangerous to come out to this place at night. Do you think you can make it back to the hotel?"

Lori's head throbbed, but the initial dizziness had gone away. "Yes, I'm sure I can. How did you happen to find me? What were you doing out here?"

"Like you, I was restless. I sometimes take long walks at night. The exercise helps me to sleep better. By chance I happened to wander out here. You can imagine my surprise when I found you unconscious. Are you sure you're all right?"

"My head hurts a little. Probably from when I hit it when I fell."

Lori felt the back of her head and winced when she

touched a swollen lump. Whoever had struck her had done a good job. Lori studied Ray Neeley's face for any giveaway signs. Even under these circumstances he was guarded and withdrawn.

"If you would let me hold your arm, I think we should be going back to the hotel," Ray said, reaching for Lori's left arm.

She really thought she could make it on her own, but she let him take her arm anyway. It would be better to go along with his wishes since she was so far from any help.

After they were a distance from the pueblo, Lori felt better. The terror she had experienced back there was beginning to fade somewhat. Still, she could not keep the unanswered questions from rising in her mind.

Who was the person she had followed into the ruins? Was it the rather somber man who walked beside her, his hand clutching her arm almost to the point of hurting her?

If the night prowler was Ray Neeley, just what was he searching for in the ruins? The hidden turquoise treasure perhaps? If this was the reason he was skulking around the deserted pueblo, then why hadn't he just hidden himself from her? No, there was some other reason why the prowler was stalking the ruins.

Lori decided to eliminate Ray Neeley as the one who had been her attacker. After all, if he were the one, he certainly wouldn't have waited around until she regained consciousness and was able to recognize him.

That only left Isabel, Mr. Owens, or Rex as possible suspects. In her heart Lori would not allow herself to believe Rex had struck her. Even though they were not as close as they had been, she still felt that he cared a little for her.

Isabel Jessop was a flamboyant, artificial person and claimed not to enjoy taking walks around the countryside. But she had been walking the day Lori picked her up upon her return from Santa Inez. So Isabel was not the hothouse type she pretended to be.

As for Oscar T. Owens, Lori wouldn't be at all surprised if the corpulent man were up to something in the ruins. All that blustery exterior might very well be a coverup.

Lori suddenly became aware that Ray Neeley had been speaking to her.

"I'm sorry, did you say something?" she asked.

"Just inquiring how you were feeling."

Lori touched the swollen area of her head and flinched. "After a good night's rest, I'm sure I'll be fine again. And I would appreciate it if you said nothing of this to my aunt."

"Why is that? I would think she would want to know about what happened to you. I mean about your taking a walk and falling."

"It would just worry Aunt Hannah. Anyway, I wasn't seriously injured."

"I hope this taught you a lesson not to go wandering around after dark by yourself. You were lucky this time."

Before Lori could check herself, she said, "Lucky? What do you mean by that remark?"

She felt Ray Neeley's strong hand tighten on her arm. "Only that you might have been seriously hurt. After all, there are dangerous places in the pueblo that you could have fallen into and nobody would know you were there."

His fingers were digging into her arm so Lori reasoned the only way she would be able to free herself of the awful pressure would be not to anger the man.

"You are right. It was foolish of me to go wandering about there by myself. It won't happen again. I can assure you of that."

These words had a soothing effect on Ray Neeley and he relaxed his tight grip on her arm.

By this time they were nearing the Crying Winds. Lori

could hardly wait until they were inside. She had to get away from this man. Ray Neeley frightened her. Even though he said he just happened to be walking past the pueblo, she did not believe him. He was quite capable of anything, even knocking her unconscious in those ruins.

Inside the hotel, Lori said a quick good night and thanked the man. Then they each went their separate ways. Lori hurried through the kitchen door. A light above the sink was still blazing and as Lori passed the countertop she saw a plate with the remains of food in it. She did not stop but hurried to her room.

After she had shed her clothing in favor of her pajamas, she lay awake with the covers drawn up to her chin. She was convinced now that someone was taking food out of the house. Her aunt just wasn't the type to indulge in late snacks. And in some way the theft of the food was connected with the night prowler who visited the deserted pueblo.

CHAPTER FIFTEEN

The next morning Lori was up early, despite the lateness of the hour when she had gone to bed. She dressed hurriedly, then started for the kitchen. The swelling on her head had gone down, even though the area was still sensitive to her touch. As she passed her aunt's room, she noticed that her aunt's door was open and the bed had been made. Apparently, Aunt Hannah was already making breakfast.

Entering the kitchen, Lori saw Aunt Hannah washing the plate she had seen last night. At her entrance Aunt Hannah sent her a quick, nervous glance.

"You're up early," Aunt Hannah said in a crisp, flat tone. "Thought I'd get breakfast going. Now that you're here, I'll leave it to you."

Hannah Hudson rinsed the plate and put it on the plastic drainer to dry. As she wiped her hands on her denim pants, she said, "I'll be in the dining room."

Trying to avert Lori's eyes, Aunt Hannah walked briskly out of the kitchen, but in doing so she had to pass Lori. The early morning light fell upon the guarded features of her aunt and Lori could not suppress the surprised gasp that passed her lips.

In the brief glimpse she had caught of her aunt she knew that these were not the features of a woman in her middle years. The skin was smooth, wrinkle-free, and youthful. Suddenly Lori knew that this woman could not be her aunt, she was far too young.

If she were not Hannah Hudson, then who was she? And what was she doing in this hotel passing herself off as Lori's aunt? Another frightened thought flared through Lori's mind. Where was the real Hannah Hudson?

For a moment Lori panicked. She thought of running out of the kitchen, away from the hotel. Away from this imposter. She even thought of going to Rex's room and telling him of her suspicions.

But she knew she could not do that. She had lost the feeling of trust that once was shared between them. All she could do was bide her time until she could discover what was going on at The House of the Crying Winds.

She was so preoccupied with her thoughts that she didn't remember fixing the waffles and sausages. It seemed a miracle to her that nothing was burned when she took the tray of food into the dining room.

Lori was relieved to find everyone at the table when she arrived with the food.

"That smells good," Rex said as he pulled out a chair next to his. For the first time in days Lori was glad to be sitting next to Rex.

"Did you sleep well, Lori?" came the affected voice of Isabel Jessop.

Lori studied the face of the fading beauty for any underlying insinuation in her question. Isabel Jessop appeared to be mildly interested in Lori and the question she had asked.

"Well enough," Lori replied. "Why did you ask?"

The actress gave an elaborate shrug of her shoulders. "You just appear somewhat pale this morning. Not your usual robust self."

Lori's emerald green eyes darted in the direction of Ray

Neeley, who was pouring syrup on his waffles. He apparently was going to make good his promise not to mention the incident at the ruins last night.

"Maybe you're working the girl too hard, Hannah," Oscar T. Owens said as he speared some sausages with his fork.

Lori shifted her gaze from Ray Neeley to the woman who sat next to the portly salesman. Once again she had become the woman Lori had first met when she arrived at the Crying Winds.

Somehow this woman—Lori could no longer think of her as Aunt Hannah—had managed to age from the time she had seen her earlier in the kitchen. It was obviously the expert application of cosmetics. That could be the only explanation for the sudden aging of this woman.

"Lori is free to go back to Ohio anytime she wants to. Far be it from me to keep her here against her wishes."

"But I don't want to go back to Ohio," Lori said emphatically. "I was hired for the summer and I intend to work until it's over. Unless you don't find my work satisfactory."

Aunt Hannah was glaring at Lori. There was a sudden silence at the table.

The silence was broken by Isabel, who said, "Personally, I think Lori's doing an admirable job. The food here is excellent. Some of the best I've tasted."

Somehow these words eased the tension between Lori and Hannah Hudson. The talk around the table became more relaxed and natural.

After breakfast everyone went their separate ways. Aunt Hannah walked to the linen closet and loaded a small pushcart with fresh linen and towels.

Lori happened to glance out the window in the living room as Rex left the house carrying his photographic equipment. He looked more handsome than ever, but there were scowl lines between his shaggy eyebrows. Lori watched him as he loaded the equipment into his truck.

She wished she could wave to him and talk about the pictures he planned on shooting that day, yet she knew it was too late for that. Since Sharon had arrived on the scene, everything had changed between her and Rex.

When he lifted his massive frame into the truck and drove away, Lori found there was a lump in her throat that was hard to swallow.

Her reverie was broken as Hannah Hudson came by wheeling the pushcart. "Getting low on supplies. I want you to take another trip into Santa Inez tomorrow."

"Very well," Lori replied.

Hannah Hudson was no longer pretending to be civil toward her. Instead of asking her to do something, she was now giving orders.

"That is unless you would like to go into town," Lori said.

"Why should I?"

"No reason. Except maybe there are some friends you might want to see. All you seem to do is work. Don't you ever get away from this place?"

Hannah Hudson fixed her emerald green eyes on Lori and her mouth twisted in a mocking sneer. "No time for my friends, as you call them. This place takes all my time and energy. Besides, I'm not a social butterfly, like my niece obviously is."

Not waiting for a reply from Lori, Hannah Hudson went over toward the guest rooms. Lori waited for a few minutes, her face aflame with anger and indignation. It was obvious that the woman was doing her best to get under Lori's skin.

All Lori had to do was complain about anything and she would be asked to leave. Lori knew now that her real Aunt

Hannah certainly would not be acting in such a manner. Who was this woman? And what was she doing in this place?

Lori knew that she could not allow herself to become overtly suspicious. If she did, she might never learn the answers to her questions. She could not go to the police with her suspicions, for that was what they were.

As of right now she had no proof that the woman was an imposter. Lori was a newcomer to the area. The authorities would surely accept Hannah Hudson's word over her own. If only there was someone she could confide in. But there was nobody, not even Rex.

"If I only had some proof," Lori said aloud.

Then an idea began to take shape. She walked in the direction of the guests' rooms and saw Hannah entering the Neeleys' room.

She should be in there for a while. That will give me time for what I want to do, Lori thought to herself.

Then Lori walked with a quickening stride to Hannah's room. The door was now closed and Lori paused before it, taking a deep breath of air. She was about to invade the privacy of her supposed aunt's room. It was something Lori had never done before.

She had never so much as read a letter that wasn't addressed to herself in her entire life. However, this was altogether different. The woman who claimed to be Hannah Hudson was an imposter. Lori had to find something to confirm her suspicions.

Reaching out, Lori touched the doorknob and cautiously turned it as she applied pressure. The door opened inwardly. Leaving the door ajar, Lori stepped into the room. She took in with a glance the row of wigs and the neat, newly made bed.

Cautiously she walked over to the low chest of drawers

and began rummaging through the drawers. Every once in a while she glanced nervously over her shoulder in case she was being observed.

The contents of the drawers offered nothing in the way of evidence she was seeking. Quickly, almost with relief, she shut them and focused her attention on a jewelry box which sat at one end of the chest of drawers.

Gingerly she opened the box. Inside she found several strands of beads and bracelets made from silver and encrusted with turquoise. There was a diamond ring in one corner of the box, which was the only piece of jewelry not fashioned from turquoise.

Closing the jewelry box, Lori wandered over to the ornate nightstand beside Hannah's bed. Taking the brass handle in her hand, she opened a small drawer. Inside lay a crumpled pack of cigarettes with a few still inside. So Aunt Hannah was a secret smoker, Lori thought, replacing the pack.

As she did this, her hand touched a smooth metal object and Lori picked it up. It was a small butane lighter. Turning it over in her hands, she saw that there were initials engraved on the front of the lighter. Lori walked over to the window where the light was better and studied the engraving. Very clearly she made out the initials C.D.O. finely etched on the metal.

C.D.O.? Those definitely were not Hannah Hudson's initials. It was possible the lighter belonged to someone else. Or the lighter might have been lent her by someone and she never got around to returning it. Lori dropped the lighter back into the drawer, then closed it.

So far she had only learned that the person pretending to be her aunt was a smoker. To Lori that was incriminating evidence since her father had told her his sister was a nonsmoker. Yet she doubted that this news would cause anyone to suspect Hannah Hudson of being anything other than who she pretended to be.

Lori drifted over to the closet, deep in thought. She idly opened the door and halfheartedly looked at the clothes that were hung there; mostly jackets and plaid shirts and a mackintosh. On the floor were several pairs of boots and some casual shoes.

In the corner she saw a small case that somehow, by the texture of the leather, appeared out of place. Lori squatted down and inspected the case. At a flick of her finger the top opened and she gazed at its contents. She had only a second to look because she heard footsteps not too far away.

Quickly Lori snapped the case shut and got to her feet. She hurried out of the room and was closing the door behind her when Aunt Hannah's voice forced her to pivot around.

"What are you up to?" came the harsh, accusing voice of Hannah Hudson.

Lori swallowed, wondering if Hannah had seen her emerge from her room. She took a chance that she hadn't. "I was going into your room to see if it might need dusting."

"Is that right? I thought I made it clear to you that I would take care of my own room. If there's any dusting to be done, I can take care of it."

"I must have forgotten. It won't happen again," Lori said, trying to keep her gaze unwavering against the dark look her aunt was giving her.

"See that it doesn't. I ran out of towels. Those Neeleys must be stealing them."

With a final appraising look, Hannah Hudson headed toward the linen closet. Lori moved quickly toward the living room and began picking up scattered newspapers and magazines.

When Hannah appeared again with an armload of towels, she said, "You could be making a list of what we need in town. Can't do everything around here."

No sooner had Hannah left than Nancy Neeley walked in the front door. Lori was on her way to the kitchen, but she paused when the surly woman spoke to her.

"Miss Hudson, I'd like to have a few words with you."

Lori did not want to talk to the disagreeable woman, but there was no way to avoid it. "Certainly. I am rather busy, though."

"This won't take a minute," Nancy Neeley said as she advanced toward Lori.

As the haughty woman drew nearer, Lori could see the anger that smoldered in her eyes.

"Last night you were with my husband. Am I correct?"

Lori was caught off guard. She hadn't expected this from Ray Neeley's wife.

"You are right. But it's not what you think. I went for a walk and I tripped over a rock. I must have struck my head. Your husband found me as I was regaining consciousness. He helped me back to the hotel."

Nancy Neeley arched a disbelieving eyebrow. "A likely story."

"Likely or not, it's the truth," Lori said, becoming angry in spite of herself. "He told me he was restless and had gone for a walk. Surely he must have said something to you before he left."

This time it was Nancy's turn to become flustered. "I must have been asleep when he left."

"Then how did you know that he returned to the hotel with me?"

"That doesn't matter. Why don't you leave this place? If I were you, I would. For your own good."

"Is that a threat?" Lori said, keeping her voice low.

"Call it what you will. Personally, I would say it was just good, sound, sensible advice."

Before Lori could say anything in return, Nancy Neeley had gone as abruptly as she had appeared. Lori clenched her fists and walked briskly to the kitchen. She had tried to explain to the woman that Ray Neeley had only been a good Samaritan. But from the look on Nancy's face, Lori knew that she did not believe her.

"Well, it was the truth. I haven't done anything wrong," Lori said half aloud and she felt better.

She couldn't help it if Nancy Neeley was consumed with jealousy. But she knew that in the future she would keep a wide berth between herself and Ray Neeley. She did not need that problem at the moment. There were enough problems as it was.

Writing down the list of supplies took Lori's mind off Ray and Nancy Neeley. She spent the better part of an hour making up the list. When she was finished, she poured herself a cup of coffee and sat down at the small kitchen table.

She touched the back of her head and found the swelling had gone down considerably. With that touch the events of the past evening came rushing back to her. She realized she was no closer to finding out who was going to the ruins at night than she had ever been.

But there was something else, something more important that she had temporarily blocked out of her head. Something she had seen in Hannah Hudson's room. Then she remembered. The case in the clothes closet. It had to be a makeup kit.

CHAPTER SIXTEEN

Off and on during the day Lori was to find herself thinking about Hannah Hudson and the contents of her room. She was grateful for her work; it kept her from dwelling too long on her suspicions.

Lunch was a quiet affair with only herself, Hannah, and Isabel Jessop eating. The Neeleys left word they would be dining in Santa Inez and Oscar T. Owens and Rex had both asked for sandwiches.

Dinner found all the guests surrounding the table. Isabel Jessop, as usual, kept the conversation flowing. While Lori was doing the dishes, Rex came in.

"Just want to tell you how much I enjoyed dinner. You outdid youself."

"Thank you. Did you have a productive day?"

"So so." Rex shrugged. "Anything I can do to help?"

Lori shook her head. "This is my job. I think I've made you aware of that in the past."

"That you have," Rex replied, leaning against the wall and studying Lori from a distance. "Is anything bothering you? You didn't have much to say at dinner."

"Everything is fine. I guess I'm just tired."

Lori avoided Rex's intense gaze. She knew that if she permitted herself, she would tell him all about her suspicions of Hannah Hudson. She no longer trusted Rex to the extent that she could confide in him. The moment passed and they went on to another subject.

Lori excused herself after she had done the dishes and did not join the others in the living room.

"I think I'll get some sleep. I'll be going to Santa Inez first thing in the morning."

Even though it was early, Lori went to sleep almost immediately. But she did not have peaceful dreams. They were troubled and fraught with frightening images.

In one she was running frantically through the dark recesses of the pueblo. The wind howled and cried dismally all around her, almost as though it were a living presence. Then she came to a decayed doorway. She stopped, trying to catch her breath.

Something moved in the murky shadows. Lori was too frightened to run or cry out. Whatever it was began to walk stealthily toward her. Moonlight fell suddenly upon the darkened area and in the pale glow she saw the hideously distorted features of Hannah Hudson moving menacingly toward her.

Lori awoke with a start. She could still see the image of her aunt as she moved toward her in the darkened ruins. Lori tossed and turned, afraid to go back to sleep, but she did.

When she opened her eyes again it was dawn. The nightmares of the previous evening somehow appeared foolish in the bright, warm glow of the sun. She hurriedly splashed cold water on her face, then put on a bright yellow linen dress. Then she looked in the mirror and found that she appeared more refreshed than she felt.

In the kitchen she made coffee and ate a slice of toast. The house was quiet at that time of day. The crying sound made by the ever-present wind had ceased. Lori walked to the kitchen window and looked out. Ahead of her stretched the stark but beautiful scenery that was New Mexico.

She had grown to love the sight of the far mountains and the deep blue sky. In a way she would be sorry when the summer had ended and she would be returning to Ohio. Not only would she miss the scenery, but she knew she would miss Rex. A lump that was almost impossible to swallow formed in her throat.

It had all been so good between her and Rex until she had seen him with Sharon. Now everything was mixed up and complicated.

"This isn't doing me any good," Lori muttered to herself. "And it certainly isn't getting the shopping done."

Turning her back on the spectacular view from the window, Lori grabbed the list she had prepared and the keys to the car.

As she entered the patio, she came to an abrupt halt. Rex Fraser was sitting in one of the patio chairs. It was too late to avoid him, so Lori nodded in his direction.

"You really meant it when you said you would be up bright and early," the blond giant said, rising to his feet.

"Of course. Are you usually up this early in the morning?"

"Not generally. Frankly, I'll have to confess I was waiting for you."

"For what reason?"

"To see that you got off safely to Santa Inez. I can promise you there was no ulterior motive."

Lori studied Rex's handsome face for a moment. Try as she would, she still could not believe what he was saying. She was angry at herself for her skepticism, yet there was nothing she could do about it.

"That was nice of you. Although I am fully capable of taking care of myself," she said, hating the tone of her voice.

"Are you certain of that?"

"Positive. Now, I really should be going. It is a rather long drive."

Rex could not conceal his disappointment. "If you insist. I hope you have a safe trip."

Lori wished he hadn't put it that way. Why shouldn't she have a safe trip? The car was in good working condition and she knew the road fairly well.

"What are your plans fo for the day?" she asked, trying to display some interest in his work.

Rex hesitated, then said, "A friend is dropping by. We're going to explore some remote area of the countryside."

From the look on Rex's face, Lori immediately knew who his friend was. The contentment she had felt earlier that morning was gone. So he and Sharon were planning on getting together. Lori couldn't bear to look at Rex any longer. She felt that if she did, he would be able to see the hurt and humiliation on her face.

"Have a good time," she said as airily as she could. "And enjoy yourself."

Before Rex could reply, she walked as fast as she could without actually breaking into a run. When she got to the garage, she slammed the door to the car and drove away in a flurry of dust. She didn't dare look at the patio for fear that Rex would see the expression on her face. Lori felt moist tears on her cheeks and wiped them away with an annoyed thrust of her hand.

She had made the mistake of falling in love with him. And it was too late to change her heart. She couldn't make herself believe that Rex didn't care a little in return. Still, there was Sharon. And where did that leave her?

Lori switched on the car radio, hoping the music would take her mind off her problems. For a while it helped.

The wind coming in the open windows was clean and

refreshing. Even though she had been on the road several times the passing countryside was still inspiring.

When her thoughts began to drift back to Rex, she fought them and instead concentrated on Aunt Hannah. Only she wasn't her aunt and Lori doubted that her name was Hannah. Whoever the woman was she was an even better actress than Isabel Jessop.

Where could her real aunt be? And what had become of her? Somehow it all seemed like a horrible nightmare. She had come all the way from Ohio to help her aunt and instead a stranger was passing herself off as Hannah Hudson.

It seemed impossible, unbelievable that this was happening. There was no way for Lori to call her parents about her suspicions. And the police, for the time being, were out of the question. It was up to her to get to the bottom of this puzzle. Lori silently prayed that her real aunt was somewhere safe and unharmed.

At the outskirts of Santa Inez, the traffic began to thicken, and Lori gave all her attention to her driving. She found the market without any difficulty and was pleasantly surprised when the checkout clerk remembered her.

"You're the one working at the Crying Winds, aren't you?" the pert, friendly girl said as she punched the cash register. "I've always wanted to see the inside of that place. Is it fancy?"

"Not really," Lori replied with a smile. "But it does have a lot of atmosphere."

"Don't you get kinda lonely out there all by yourself?"

"I don't have time. Besides, there are other people staying at the hotel."

"Sure. And then there's your aunt. Still, it is a long way from civilization. Me, I like to be around a lot of people. Not that Santa Inez is such a thriving metropolis."

As Lori was leaving the market, she saw a woman

hurrying toward her, waving one arm in greeting. It was Bessie.

"Oh, Lori, I'm so glad I ran into you," Bessie puffed, out of breath. "I was afraid I wouldn't see you before I left."

"You're leaving? Is anything the matter?" Lori asked with concern.

"Nothing to get all worked up about. I have some property in Albuquerque and I have to go back home to sign some papers. Legal stuff, you know."

Lori breathed a sigh of relief, although she would miss the pleasant, honest woman. In the short time she'd known Bessie, she had become fond of her.

"When do you leave?" Lori asked.

"In about an hour or so. Do you have time for a cup of coffee? There's a nice little cafe next to the market."

The cafe was clean and small and they were the only customers. A middle-aged waitress with a wry sense of humor took their order, then went away leaving them alone.

"How are things at the hotel? Are you enjoying your work?"

Lori decided to tell Bessie everything. She needed someone to confide in. After all, the woman would be leaving in an hour, and what harm would it do? She spoke about being locked in the linen closet, of her following the mysterious person to the ruins and being struck on the head. As she spoke, Bessie sipped her coffee, her eyes never leaving Lori's face.

"Then I found the makeup kit in Aunt Hannah's room. I'm almost positive it was the one stolen from Isabel Jessop's car."

"So you think this woman who calls herself Hannah Hudson is not really your aunt?" Bessie finally managed to say.

"She's really not as old as she appears. With a wig and professional makeup she is passing as a much older person."

Bessie swallowed a sip of coffee, then said, "But why is she doing this? If she's not your aunt, then where is the real Hannah Hudson?"

"There are so many unanswered questions. But I don't plan on leaving the Crying Winds until I find the answers. Even if it means confronting that woman face to face with what I've learned."

"She could be dangerous," Bessie warned. "Why don't you turn the whole thing over to the authorities? I'm frightened for you, Lori."

"I thought about that, but I really don't have enough evidence to accuse my aunt, or rather this woman, whoever she is."

Bessie gave a deep sigh. "At least you have that nice Mr. Fraser to help you. I won't worry so much about you if he's around."

Lori refrained from telling Bessie about Sharon. If Bessie knew that Rex had been seeing the beautiful brunette, and that there was a strained relationship between herself and Rex, it would only upset her. Bessie was a goodhearted person and she had her own problems. Lori wanted her to go away thinking everything was all right between herself and Rex.

With a quick glance at her wristwatch, Bessie shoved the cup of coffee aside. "Didn't realize it was getting so late. Now, Lori, here's my address in Albuquerque," she said, fishing through her purse. "Please let me know how this all comes out. My heavens, it's just like a mystery story. You take care now. And, for my sake, don't take any foolish chances."

Lori hugged Bessie and there were tears in both their eyes as Bessie hurried out of the cafe. In just the brief time they had known each other, a strong friendship had grown between them. Lori made a mental note to stop off in Albuquerque and see Bessie before she returned to Ohio.

After Bessie had gone, Lori sat at the table with the cup of coffee the waitress had replenished. She had to be getting back to The House of the Crying Winds. But before she went, this was the time she must think of some way to expose the woman who was posing as her aunt. When she was talking with Bessie, the thought had been expressed that she confront the woman at the Crying Winds with her suspicions. Perhaps this might not be such a bad idea. The element of surprise, catching the imposter off guard. But it would have to be the right time and the right place.

Paying the waitress, Lori returned to her car. It was nearing the lunch hour, but Lori was not hungry. She could always fix herself a light snack when she got back to the hotel.

It didn't take long to reach the outskirts of Santa Inez, which was a small but picturesque town. It was the kind of town that Lori could easily adapt to since her own hometown in Ohio wasn't that much larger.

You have to finish college, and what would there be here for you? she thought to herself, realizing that she had been allowing her fantasies to get out of hand.

Once this matter at the Crying Winds was settled, she would be returning to Ohio. There would be nothing, nor anyone to keep her in New Mexico. For a fleeting moment she thought about Rex and how much she loved him. These thoughts were too painful and she managed to shake them off, although it was not an easy task to accomplish.

Now that she was outside the town, the road gradually grew steeper. Lori glanced in the rearview mirror and saw a car some distance behind her. Giving it a casual glance, she concentrated on the road ahead, which now was serpentine, twisting into dangerous curves.

Lost in her concentration, she had forgotten the vehicle behind her until she came to a straight stretch of road. Out of habit she looked into the rearview mirror and saw that the car had gained on her and was traveling at a high rate of speed. Lori instinctively moved toward the right, for it was evident the car was going to pass her own vehicle.

The other car was gaining on her. Lori fought the wheel to keep as near the right-hand side of the road as possible.

Why doesn't he pass me? Lori wondered as the right tires on the car skimmed off the pavement, sending a shower of dust into the air. She didn't dare venture a quick glance into the rearview mirror for fear of losing control and overcorrecting. Suddenly the other vehicle moved alongside of her own.

Instead of accelerating and passing, it nudged her vehicle. Lori realized with panic that the other car was forcing her off the road. Frantically she looked to the right and saw a turnoff not far ahead. If she could only make it that far. She held her breath as the turnoff neared, and then she turned to the right.

The other car roared on by, but not before Lori got a good look at the driver. It was Oscar T. Owens.

CHAPTER SEVENTEEN

Lori applied the brakes and the car skidded to a stop in a burst of sand and dust. Her hands clenched the steering wheel until her knuckles ached. The car which had forced her off the road had disappeared around a curve in the distance. A car whose driver was Oscar T. Owens.

She could still see the pudgy face as it looked with a mocking grin on its lips as she was forced off the road. Why had Oscar done this to her? Had he been following her ever since she had gone to Santa Inez? Just waiting for the chance to harm her? Like so many of the things that had happened to her since she had arrived at the hotel, this did not make sense.

It was true that she did not care much for the beefy salesman, yet she had never been deliberately unkind to the man. Not unkind enough to provoke this attack upon herself. There had been no reason for him to force her off the road. Just the thought of what he had done brought angry tears to Lori's eyes. Well, whatever Oscar's motives were she aimed to find out.

Waiting a few moments longer until she felt her self-control returning, Lori released the emergency brake and was back on the road. She did not see Oscar's car ahead; he had been given enough leeway by her stopping to have driven out of sight.

149

Lori drove rapidly but at a safe speed all the way back to the hotel. One brush with an accident was enough for one day.

When she arrived at the Crying Winds, she parked the car in the garage and took the purchases into the house. As she angrily stacked the canned goods on a shelf, she thought about going directly to Mr. Owens's room and accusing him of what he had attempted to do to her.

Then she thought better of that. There would be a better time when everyone was assembled at the dinner table. Somehow she wanted to see how he would react in front of other witnesses.

All that afternoon Lori's thoughts were directed toward the fat salesman. She spent the better part of the day cleaning up the living room, although it really did not need much attention.

At one point Nancy Neeley came in, but when she saw Lori, she turned abruptly and left the room. Lori was annoyed that Nancy felt this way toward her. Maybe in time she would forget all about seeing her husband and Lori together. Lori hated to think of leaving the hotel with Nancy harboring such mistaken ideas about her.

At four o'clock Isabel Jessop walked into the living room. "A tomb. This place is quiet as a tomb. Ah, Lori! At least you liven this place up somewhat."

"Would you care for a cup of coffee? I was just going to take a break."

"Excellent idea. I'll be on the patio."

If it were anyone but Isabel Jessop, Lori would have resented being treated in such a manner. As it was Lori shook her head and with a slight smile went into the kitchen and emerged with two cups of coffee.

As usual, Isabel had taken the lounging chair and was reclining like the Queen of the Nile. Lori handed her a cup and took a seat opposite the actress.

"You were out rather late last night, weren't you?" Isabel asked, her watery eyes looking at Lori above the rim of the cup.

"As a matter of fact, I was. How did you know?"

"I saw you coming back to the hotel. My insomnia, you know. You weren't alone, either."

Lori put her cup on the patio end table. "You have very good eyesight. I should tell you I was with Ray Neeley."

The actress's eyebrows fluttered with interest. Then Lori told her about going to the ruins and falling and hitting her head.

When she got to the part about Ray Neeley finding her, Isabel arched a dubious eyebrow. "Quite a coincidence, isn't it? He just happened to be walking past the pueblo. Really, Lori, you can do better than that."

"It's the truth," Lori said. Then she showed Isabel where she had been struck on the head.

"You are telling the truth. I'd hardly think you would go to all the trouble to substantiate your story. Well, let this be a lesson to you. Don't go wandering around those ruins after dark."

Lori assured the actress that she would not. They finished their coffee, then Isabel left. After Isabel had gone, Lori went to her room and took a quick shower and put on her denims and a paisley shirt.

In the kitchen she baked some pork chops and cooked some fresh green beans. That, with a nice tossed salad, should be enough for dinner, Lori thought.

It was six o'clock. Lori glanced at the wall clock in the kitchen as she heard the telephone ringing at the desk. She hurried from the kitchen and stopped abruptly when she saw Aunt Hannah reach for the phone.

"I'll get it," came the stentorian voice of the woman posing as her aunt.

Lori was about to return to the kitchen when she heard

her aunt say, "Mr. Fraser? I'll see if he's in his room."

Hannah Hudson placed the receiver on the desk and with a cynical raise of her eyebrows said, "A woman calling for Rex. He does get around."

Trying not to show her disappointment Lori quickly turned and went back into the kitchen. She heard the loud footsteps as Hannah hurried to call Rex to the telephone. Lori felt that the only person on the end of the line could be Sharon.

She busied herself in the kitchen so that she could not hear Rex when he came to answer the phone. This was too much for her to take. Then with a sigh she realized Rex could talk to whomever he pleased. She wasn't the only woman in New Mexico that he knew. This should have helped her, but it didn't.

At dinner that night she found herself being seated next to Rex. The blond giant was charming and as attentive as ever and for a brief time she found herself forgetting about Sharon and what she obviously meant to the photographer.

Oscar T. Owens was late arriving and was his usual blustering self. He appeared as though nothing had happened that afternoon on the road. Lori found herself glaring at the corpulent man.

It was Isabel who first spoke to the salesman.

"You're late tonight, Mr. Owens. Been out selling the Brooklyn Bridge?"

Oscar grunted and ignored the remark as he reached for the pork chops and loaded his plate. "Business was good. I only just got back."

That was all Lori needed. "Are you sure, Mr. Owens? I could have sworn I ran into you on the road from Santa Inez. Or was it the other way around?"

She watched the man's face for a telltale sign of guilt. But Oscar T. Owens displayed no emotion. Only, his hands clenched tightly on his knife and fork.

"I don't know what you are talking about. As far as Santa Inez is concerned, I was nowhere near that place today."

Rex had been listening intently. Now he said, "What's all this about running into somebody? You didn't have another accident, did you, Lori?"

Lori did not take her eyes off Oscar T. Owens. "It wasn't an accident. Someone deliberately tried to run me off the road. It was in the hills outside Santa Inez. If it hadn't been for the turnoff, there would have been an accident."

Isabel Jessop dropped her fork. The drama of the situation had gotten to her. "That's horrible. Did you happen to see who was driving the other car?"

"It was all very sudden, but I did manage to look in that direction. The driver bore a remarkable resemblance to Mr. Owens."

"That will be enough of that, Lori," Hannah Hudson said in her stern voice. "You should be more careful what you say."

"Do you think you might have been mistaken?" Isabel asked. "After all, it all happened so quickly."

Lori had accomplished what she had intended. Oscar T. Owens was glowering at her with such a look of hatred that she knew she had been right. And he knew that she had recognized him.

"It's possible. So why don't we just forget the whole thing? I'm sorry I brought it up. Anyway, neither the car nor myself were harmed."

Even though Lori had tried to dismiss the near accident, her words settled like a pall over the dining table. Isabel tried valiantly to interject some wit, but everyone appeared to be absorbed in his own thoughts. As a last resort, Isabel suggested they play a game of cards after dinner and this was met with a halfhearted enthusiasm.

While Lori was in the kitchen, Rex came in. His thick, bushy eyebrows were drawn tightly together with deep concern.

"Why didn't you tell me what happened to you on the way home? You could have been seriously injured."

"I could have, but I wasn't. Anyway, does it really matter to you?"

Rex put his strong hands on her shoulders and turned her toward him. "Of course, it matters to me. It matters very much."

Lori wished in her heart that she could believe him. There was a time when she would have; now there were lingering doubts.

"I'm not so certain it does. After all, we've only known each other a short time. And I feel there could be someone else you're concerned about."

The scowl lines between Rex's brows deepened.

"By that remark you could only be referring to Sharon."

"You said her name, not me."

"Listen, Lori, you must trust me. What's between Sharon and myself is something I can't talk about. Not now, anyway."

Lori moved away from Rex's strong hands. "Let's join the others, shall we?"

Rex stared at her for a moment and then gave a resigned shrug of his massive shoulders. "Suit yourself."

The Neeleys had retired for the evening, which left only five people at the table. Lori thought the evening would never end. Occasionally she glanced into Rex's eyes, but he shifted his gaze to the cards he held in his hands. She could still hear the words he had spoken earlier in the kitchen. He as much as said that there was something between him and Sharon.

At ten o'clock, Oscar T. Owens put his cards on the

table and said, "Deal me out. I've had a long day. I'm going to bed."

No sooner had he gone than Isabel complained of a headache, and she made an exit that would have done justice to Camille. While Lori and Rex were talking, Hannah slipped away unnoticed.

"About what I said earlier this evening," Rex began, but Lori stopped him.

"It isn't necessary for you to explain anything. After all, you are a guest here and I am only an employee."

Rex's eyes flared as he got to his feet. "Have it that way, if you want. You are the most unreasonable person I have ever met in my entire life."

Without another word, Rex stomped angrily out of the room, leaving Lori staring blankly after him. So she was unreasonable, was she? What about him and his clandestine phone calls? Lori didn't know whether to become angry or hurt.

All she knew was that Rex was slowly growing further and further away from her. She wouldn't be surprised if he never spoke to her again. But there was nothing she could do. Sharon would always be there between the two of them.

Lori knew she would have a difficult time getting to sleep, so she decided a glass of warm milk might help. Her eyes were misting over and she knew that it wouldn't take much to bring on tears. She wished she had never come to New Mexico. She wished she was with her parents in Europe.

Catching herself with these thoughts brought her up suddenly. Was that all the spunk she had? At the first sign of disappointment, all she thought about was running like a scared rabbit back to the safety of her parents.

Well, she wouldn't do that! She couldn't do that. No

matter what the circumstances were here, no matter how unpleasant, she would stick it out until summer was over.

She was rubbing her eyes when she entered the kitchen and so at first she wasn't certain what she saw was real. Standing at the counter, her wig resting on a chair, was Hannah Hudson. No, this flame-haired person was not her aunt.

Gone was any pretense that she was Lori's aunt. She turned away from the food she had been preparing on a dish and faced Lori with a mocking grin.

"So you've decided to come out of hiding," Lori said, the tears gone from her emerald green eyes.

"That's right. And I can't say I'll miss that thing," she said, nodding toward the wig. "It was like wearing a skull-cap all day. You don't seem surprised, little niece."

Lori moved tentatively toward the woman. "I'm not. I've thought for some time that you weren't my aunt. And when I found the makeup kit in your room, I was certain of it."

A cruel grin touched the corners of the woman's mouth. "I thought you had been snooping around in my room. You know what they say about curiosity and the cat."

"This is no time for games. I want to know who you are and what you are doing here. What have you done with my aunt?"

The woman wasn't the least bit intimidated by Lori or her questions. Now that the wig was gone and the pretense no longer necessary, the woman who had been playing the role of Hannah Hudson had become hard as granite.

"You'll find out. All in good time."

Lori took a few more steps forward. The eyes of the imposter were wary, waiting for any unexpected move on Lori's part.

"I want to know now. You can't get away with whatever

you have in mind. I'll telephone the authorities if you don't answer some questions."

The eyes of the imposter hardened. "That wouldn't be advisable if you want your aunt returned alive and well."

Suddenly Lori was aware of the position she had placed herself in. If this woman held Hannah captive someplace, she could blackmail Lori into meeting whatever demands she made. The threat of the police held no terror for this hardened woman.

"Where have you taken my aunt? Can I see her?"

The woman nodded her head slowly. "Sooner than you think. That is if you mind your manners and don't try anything foolish."

"That food you were preparing, is that for my aunt?"

Again the woman nodded.

"Then it was you I have been seeing every night going to the pueblo. You have been taking food to my aunt. That means she's somewhere in the pueblo."

"You catch on quick. Only last night you got a little too close for comfort and something had to be done about your interfering."

Lori automatically touched the sore spot on her head. Then it had been this woman who had chased her from the ruins and attacked her when she tripped over the rock.

"No sense in jabbering all night. Here, you take the plate. We're going for a little walk."

"If I refuse?" Lori said.

The woman withdrew her hand, which she had kept concealed behind her back. Lori looked into the blackened barrel of a gun.

CHAPTER EIGHTEEN

Lori could not believe this was actually happening to her, that this was real—not just a horrible dream. Then the woman made a gesture with the gun, indicating the plate of food.

"You want to see your aunt, don't you?"

Lori nodded meekly.

"Then pick up that food. It's getting late."

While Lori moved toward the counter, the woman reached into a drawer with her free hand and removed a flashlight. Standing behind Lori, she nudged her with the barrel of the gun.

"Hurry up. I don't like being in that pueblo after dark any more than you do."

"Is that where you've taken my aunt?"

"Where else?"

Lori felt the hard muzzle of the gun against the small of her back as she walked out of the house. Even though the night was cool, she felt droplets of perspiration on her forehead. She clutched the plate of food tightly in her hands, which were beginning to tremble.

Once outside, they circled the hotel, until they were on the pathway leading to the distant ruins. By now the woman was almost walking abreast of Lori so that she could shine the flashlight on the crude pathway.

Lori had glanced at Rex's windows as they had passed his room. The room was darkened, indicating that Rex was undoubtedly asleep. She wished that she had not been so rude to him earlier; he might have stayed with her. Then all of this would have been avoided. Now there was no way she could call on him for help.

"Watch what you're doing," came the sharp voice of the woman bringing Lori back from her reverie. "Unless you want your aunt to eat sand tonight, you'd better not drop that dish."

Poor Aunt Hannah, Lori thought. What she must be going through all alone out there in the pueblo. How long had she been held captive? And for what reason? Did it have anything to do with the buried turquoise?

Perhaps this woman thought Aunt Hannah knew the whereabouts of the treasure and was trying to force her into telling where it was buried. That had to be the reason behind all this. Nothing else made sense.

"Stop dawdling and keep moving," the woman said. "I don't want to be out here all night."

"I'm moving as fast as I can. By the way, what is your name? It's obvious I can't keep calling you Aunt Hannah."

There was a mocking laugh from the woman. "Aunt Hannah! I'm no more your aunt than one of those jack-rabbits is your uncle. Call me Camilla."

"Is that your real name?"

"Believe it or not it is."

"Are you from New Mexico? Were you born here?"

Again Camilla snorted. "You must be joking. This is the first time I have ever been in this state. And I hope I never see it again. When this is over I'm heading for San Francisco."

"And you plan on taking the turquoise with you. Is that the idea?"

"Turquoise? What turquoise?"

"Isn't that why you're holding my aunt captive, so that she will tell you where the turquoise is buried?"

"There isn't any turquoise buried out there. That was just a legend. You've got it all wrong."

Lori paused for a moment and Camilla swept the light in her face. "What are you up to? Keep moving."

Camilla raised her other hand, the hand that held the gun. Lori had almost forgotten Camilla had the weapon.

"If it's money you need, I could get it from my parents," Lori said as she continued to walk.

"Not the kind of money I need. Besides, your aunt told me all about you and your parents. They're not that wealthy or anything."

So Camilla had forced Aunt Hannah to talk. From all Lori had heard about her aunt, that would take some doing. Aunt Hannah was a rugged and hearty person, not easily intimidated. It was hard to believe that she could be cowed by Camilla. Lori had to keep Camilla talking; perhaps she could come up with a way to escape and maybe get back to the hotel. Rex would help her then, she felt certain.

"If it isn't the turquoise, then you are after my aunt's money. How do you intend getting it?"

"That's my problem. Only it isn't going to be a problem in a little while. Even though your aunt has never met you, you are still her kin. She wouldn't want anything to happen to you. As a matter of fact, she'd give anything not to have that happen."

Goose flesh dotted Lori's arms when she heard Camilla speak. She had walked into a trap baited with Aunt Hannah. Camilla must have known she would come into the kitchen and she had been prepared. Otherwise, why would she have had the gun with her?

"You won't get away with this," Lori said without conviction.

"I think so. Who knows you're out here? If we were

seen leaving, it would just appear that we were taking a little walk before going to bed."

Of course, Camilla was right. There was nothing suspicious in their actions and she was firmly convinced no one had seen them leave the Crying Winds.

"Was it you who took Isabel Jessop's makeup kit? The one she said was stolen the night she came to the hotel?"

Camilla walked for a few minutes before answering. The gun never wavered in her grasp.

"That was easy. She had wired ahead for reservations and her room was unlocked so that she didn't have to register until later. That gave me time to make up my face before she came to the desk. Isabel was the first to arrive. After that the other guests were no problem. To them I was Hannah Hudson, owner of The House of the Crying Winds."

Camilla must have arrived when the hotel was empty and overpowered Aunt Hannah. Then she had taken her to the pueblo. Somehow it all seemed a trifle difficult for one person to handle, even though Camilla was younger than her aunt.

"Did you lock me in the linen closet that day?" Lori asked.

"That's right. The mask should have been enough to frighten you away, but you didn't scare easy. So I watched you that day you were counting linens. You almost caught me. Then Rex Fraser came along and let you out."

Lori glared at Camilla for a moment. "I could have suffocated in there."

"I doubt that. Anyway, I would have let you out. You had to leave the place. With you out of the way, Hannah Hudson would be easier to deal with."

"When I didn't leave, then you had to make other plans, is that it?"

"Things have a way of working out. If you wouldn't

be frightened away, then you could be used to get the money. You really should have gone back to Ohio."

Lori saw that they would soon be nearing the ruins. In a short time she would be seeing her aunt for the first time, but the circumstances were not what she had expected when she first arrived in New Mexico.

"What happens to me and Aunt Hannah after you get the money?"

"You won't be of any further use."

Lori didn't like the tone of Camilla's voice. "Will you let us go?"

"That all depends. You can both recognize me. It wouldn't be very smart to leave witnesses."

Instinctively Lori glanced at Camilla and in the light cast by the moon she saw the hard, cynical lines in the woman's face.

At that moment Lori knew that Camilla was capable of anything. She decided not to continue along this line of thinking. Lori did not want to put any ideas in the woman's head. She still was playing for time, hoping that she could find a way to get away from Camilla.

"How did you happen to choose the Crying Winds? Was it just by chance you came here?"

Camilla's ironic laugh filled the chill night air.

"Honey, I don't leave anything to chance. This place was studied and watched a good two months before the plan went into action."

"The plan? What plan?"

"No reason you shouldn't know since I doubt that you'll be talking much when this is all over. Now that your aunt has fixed up the Crying Winds, it can bring a handsome profit when it's sold. What with the price of real estate being what it is these days."

Lori couldn't help but gasp at what Camilla was saying.

"Aunt Hannah would never sell this place. And she certainly wouldn't give it away."

"You think not. When a person is half starved and been kept in a dark place for a long time, not to mention the threat of harm to a relative, they will do anything."

"How cruel! You've been starving my aunt! She's never done anything to you!"

"It wouldn't have been necessary if she would have cooperated in the first place."

Lori had a mental picture of her aunt shut away in a dark, dismal place. Anger against such barbaric actions flared within her.

As they neared the ruins Lori thought it must have been the moonlight playing tricks on her for she thought she saw a shadow move in a clump of bushes near the entrance to the pueblo. She dismissed it as a trick of her imagination.

When they arrived at the pueblo, Camilla said, "This place gives me the creeps. I'll be glad when this is all over and I never have to see the hotel or this place again."

Camilla lowered the gun as she moved the flashlight over the decaying walls of the pueblo. At that instant someone moved out of the night and grabbed the gun from Camilla's hand and then clamped a hand over her mouth.

The flashlight dropped and Lori bent down to retrieve it. She played the beam of light on Camilla as the woman struggled in the grasp of Rex Fraser.

"Rex! I've never been so glad to see anyone in my entire life."

"Are you all right, Lori?" came Rex's deep, reassuring voice.

"Just fine. It's Aunt Hannah I'm worried about. This woman is an imposter. Her name's Camilla and she has Aunt Hannah locked up somewhere in the pueblo."

Camilla continued to struggle in Rex's arms. Lori realized suddenly that the light was blinding Rex and she moved it quickly away from his face.

"If you'll behave I'll let go of your mouth," Rex said and this had a calming effect on Camilla.

"That's better," Rex said as he held Camilla's gun with confidence.

"How did you know we were out here?" Lori asked.

"I followed you. When I saw this red hair, at first I thought it was Isabel Jessop. Then I knew that she wasn't about to go roaming around at night. So I had a hunch you might be in trouble."

Camilla was suddenly very quiet. The anger in her eyes made them glisten in the pale light cast by the moon.

"Where have you hidden Lori's aunt?" Rex demanded. "And what do you intend doing with her?"

"You're such a smart guy, why don't you figure it out for yourself?"

"Her name is Camilla. Anyway, that's the name she gave me," Lori said.

"Very well, Camilla, or whatever your name is, you're taking us to Hannah Hudson. And no tricks."

Rex moved toward Camilla and prodded her with the gun. At first Camilla stood her ground, defiantly. Then she could tell from the look on Rex's face that he meant what he had said. A change came over Camilla and she shrugged her shoulders.

"Why not? You'll probably eventually find her yourselves. Anyway she isn't hurt. Maybe a little hungry, but she always got one meal a day."

Lori cringed at the callousness of Camilla. Even though her aunt was independent and self-sufficient, she was still not a young person. No telling what effects this experience might have on her.

"Sounds to me as though you are stalling for time," Rex said in a hard, even voice. "Hannah Hudson has suffered enough. You lead us to her, right now."

Lori was startled by the commanding tone in Rex's voice. Gone was the breezy, easygoing man she had known. Camilla, too, sensed the change and it had a surprising effect on her. She turned abruptly and walked into the ruins with Rex behind her.

Bringing up the rear and holding the flashlight with one hand, the plate of food in the other, Lori was too busy concentrating on what she was doing to see the person who slipped out of the shadows. Suddenly she felt the cold muzzle of a gun at the back of her head.

"Drop the gun, Fraser," came a voice behind her as she froze. "If you don't want any harm to come to your girlfriend you'll do as I say."

Rex whirled around as Camilla moved quickly away from him.

"Owens! I thought you were involved in all of this," Rex said, still holding the gun.

"I said drop the gun. Or don't you care what happens to Miss Hudson?"

Rex's face displayed no emotion, yet Lori could sense that he felt he had been tricked by Camilla. Slowly he lowered his arm and the gun slipped from his hand landing with a dull thud on the sandy soil.

Without a word Camilla quickly recovered the weapon. She sauntered toward Lori and wrenched the flashlight from her hand.

"That's better," came the voice of Oscar T. Owens. "I always like the odds to be on my side."

"Just as you had them on your side in Colorado and Oregon. Not to mention that widow in Mississippi," Rex said.

"How did you know about that?" asked Oscar.

"I know. I've been following your movements for some time now."

Camilla snorted, "He's a cop. I might have known that he would be."

Lori couldn't believe what she was hearing. Nothing made sense. All she knew for certain was that she was standing in the middle of a desolate pueblo and the plate of food was getting cold in her hands.

"I'm glad that my wife and I have been of such an interest to you," Oscar said.

"Your wife?" Lori blurted out.

"That's right, honey," came the smug voice of Camilla. "I'm Mrs. Oscar T. Owens. We're a team."

"A crooked team," Rex said. "We know your modus operandi. Find a wealthy widow and swindle her out of her money, then disappear. Only this time she wasn't a widow. Am I right, Mr. Owens?"

Oscar T. Owens laughed harshly. "You've got your facts pretty straight, for a policeman."

"Up till now you haven't resorted to kidnapping. In the past you've played it pretty cool. What changed your tactics this time, Owens?"

"The old lady didn't see things our way. She wouldn't deed over the property to us. So we had to persuade her that it would be to her best advantage."

"You'll make a mistake, all criminals do," Rex said with a mocking grin on his face.

"I would say you were the one who made the mistake. After all we not only have Hannah Hudson and her niece, but now you as well."

CHAPTER NINETEEN

The silence that followed Oscar's remark was only interrupted by the sighing of the evening breeze.

Lori looked at Rex Fraser. He was no longer the casual,
freelance photographer she had met when she first arrived
in Santa Inez.

He was a policeman. All the time he had been on assignment. On assignment to apprehend Oscar and Camilla
Owens. From the little she had been able to garner from
their conversation, the Owenses were con artists. She had
heard of such people who attached themselves to lonely,
gullible women and ended up absconding with their
money. She understood Rex somewhat better now.

He had known all along that Camilla was not Hannah
Hudson but rather the wife of Oscar T. Owens. Saying he
was a photographer was just a coverup for his true profes-
sion.

Now the two men faced each other. There was no fear
in Rex's eyes, only a watchful wariness.

To break up the silence, Lori said, "Was it you who
tried to frighten me away that first night by wearing the
mask?"

Oscar, who had moved away from Lori but still held
the gun levelly on her replied, "Of course. Camilla was
in another part of the house, so that she wouldn't be under

suspicion. All I had to do was slip off the mask after you screamed and come around to the front door. In all the confusion I knew that nobody would pay any attention to me.

Lori wanted to keep the beefy man talking; perhaps if he relaxed his guard, Rex might be able to overpower him. However, there was still Camilla to contend with.

"Who struck me last night when I went to the ruins? It was probably you, Mr. Owens, hiding in the shadows."

"Camilla was with your aunt. I needed to lure you away from the hiding place. When you started to run, I followed you. After you fell I thought you might recognize me, so I had to take drastic measures."

"You might have killed me."

Oscar T. Owens shrugged. "You were warned to leave the hotel. Besides, you were becoming too curious about things. We couldn't let anything interfere with our plans. Now that Hannah Hudson was beginning to weaken."

"Violence was never the way you operated before," Rex said.

"I keep forgetting that you have developed quite an interest in my career," Oscar said.

"If you want to call it that." Rex spat out the words.

Oscar did not appear to be angered by Rex's statement. He knew that he held the upper hand and there was nothing Rex could do about it.

"Why are we all standing around here?" Camilla said. "Is this some kind of a high school reunion? Let's get this over with."

Oscar smiled at the impatient Camilla. "All in good time, my dear. After all, this will probably be the last time Mr. Fraser and I will be having a social chat. Or Miss Hudson, for that matter."

Lori didn't like the ominous overtones in what Oscar had said. She was fully aware now of how dangerous this couple could be. After they had gotten the hotel from Aunt Hannah, there was nothing to prevent them from doing whatever they chose to Aunt Hannah, herself, and Rex. She knew they were capable of anything.

"You two can chat when we get to the kiva," Camilla said. "Are you coming?"

Camilla had started to walk away, so Oscar made a motion with his weapon that Rex and Lori should follow. Oscar stayed directly behind Lori to prevent Rex from making any hasty move to disarm Camilla.

The kiva, Lori thought. So that was where they had hidden Aunt Hannah. A chill tingled up her spine when she thought of the underground ceremonial chamber. How awful it must have been for Aunt Hannah to be alone down there all this time.

She prayed that her father's sister was well and not too badly damaged by the experience she had been going through. When she got out of all this, Oscar and Camilla would surely have to pay for all the misery they had inflicted on her aunt.

When she got away! Lori pondered those words over in her mind. Before she had thought Rex might be able to help her out of this dreadful situation, but now he was caught inexorably in the web spun by the Owenses as surely as she herself.

Their footsteps echoed dully as they neared the rim of the kiva. Above them the bright light from the moon showered the ruins with an eerie glow.

When they arrived at the kiva, Oscar took Camilla's flashlight. "Keep your eye on these two and don't hesitate to use that gun if they try anything."

"Don't worry, I know how to use this thing," Camilla said huskily.

Lori watched as Oscar slipped over the rim of the kiva and began moving something about in the shadowy darkness. She glanced once at Rex who flashed her a reassuring smile. Lori smiled back, but there was no confidence in the smile. In a brief time they would be joining her aunt in the lower depths of the kiva. Then what?

Oscar played the beam of light up to the rim of the kiva. "Bring them down, Camilla," he commanded.

"You heard him. Get a move on," Camilla said as she nudged Lori with her weapon.

"It's going to be all right," Rex said as he gently touched Lori's arm.

"Move," Camilla's voice cut through the silence of the night.

Lori followed Rex into the kiva, where they entered a low opening which led to a narrow passageway. It was dark and close; Lori fought the panicky feeling which was beginning to form in the pit of her stomach. It was all she could do to keep from turning and trying to make a break for it.

Somehow the passageway ended and she found herself in a circular room. It was bare except for a table on which a lamp glowed dimly. In a chair next to the table Lori saw a woman bound and gagged. Lori's eyes met the woman's and there was instant recognition. It was Aunt Hannah.

Not caring what happened to her, Lori rushed to her aunt and began untying the gag from her mouth. As she slipped the ragged strip of cloth from her aunt's mouth, Lori felt strong hands grab her shoulders.

"Aunt Hannah, it's me, Lori," she managed to cry out.

Aunt Hannah smiled wanly. "Thank heavens you're all right, Lori. These two characters tried their darnedest to get me to sign over my property to them. But they didn't reckon on me being so mule stubborn."

"Shall I put the gag back on her?" Camilla said to Oscar, who was still holding Lori by the shoulders.

"No, let the old lady talk," Oscar said. "After all, what harm can it do?"

With that Lori felt Oscar's hands loosen their grasp and she moved toward Rex.

"Are you feeling all right, Aunt Hannah?" Lori asked.

"Nothing that a good square meal won't cure. Can't complain about the food, it's been real tasty, what little there was of it. But the service is awful."

Lori suddenly remembered the plate of food that she had placed on the table. Without asking she untied the rope that bound her aunt to the chair.

Hannah Hudson rubbed her hands for a few moments, then said, "That's better. Get kinda stiff being cramped in one position all day."

There was nothing wrong with Hannah Hudson's appetite, Lori observed as the woman began devouring the food.

As she ate she glanced up at Rex and said, "He one of them?"

Lori shook her head. "No. He's staying at the hotel. He's helped me a lot. His name is Rex Fraser." She decided not to mention the fact that Rex was connected with the authorities. He had come to her rescue only to be trapped by Oscar.

"Fine-looking guy. You two going steady?"

Lori found that at a time like this and under the circumstances, she was actually blushing.

"We're friends," Lori said quickly. After all, there was still the overshadowing presence of Sharon.

"Too bad. You two make a nice-looking couple."

Camilla was growing impatient again. "This isn't getting us anywhere. Oscar, you told me this would be the last time we were coming to this hovel."

Even Oscar was beginning to get a little irritated with

his wife. "Calm down. Nobody is going anywhere. Hannah knows why we are here."

In order to delay things, Lori said, "Did you lose your pin, Aunt Hannah? A turquoise pin, shaped like a bird. I found one outside the ruins."

"It wasn't lost. I deliberately dropped it hoping that someone would find it and start asking questions. What a twist of fate. My own niece finding my pin."

"When Camilla denied it was hers, I had a feeling she was not who she pretended to be. That was confirmed by a friend in Santa Inez who recognized the pin."

Oscar looked askance at his wife.

"How was I to know the old woman had that pin? All I was supposed to do was look like her. Not be like her. And that gave me enough to do—getting the green contact lenses and everything."

"We'll talk about that later," Oscar said with a wave of his hand.

"How is the hotel going, Lori?" Aunt Hannah asked. "I've been sitting here fretting about the place ever since these two hoodlums barged in on me and took over."

Lori reassured her aunt that the Crying Winds was doing all right. She told her about Isabel Jessop and the Neeleys.

"An actress! Staying at my place. Now that's really something."

"Talk! Talk! Talk!" Camilla said between clenched teeth.

Lori noticed that Rex had been edging closer to the table while all the conversation was going on. As she looked into his eyes, she saw that they shifted their gaze to the lamp on the table and back to her again.

He did this several times as though he were trying to tell her something. Then Lori understood what he had in mind. If he could knock over the lamp, then they might have a chance of escaping in the darkness.

Camilla had moved to where she was standing almost side by side with her husband. Lori was fixing their position in her mind in case Rex's plan worked.

"I guess you're right," Oscar said in exasperation. "We'd better get this business over with."

Aunt Hannah, who had also been watching Rex, made an attempt to get up. "I've been sitting here so long I think my feet have taken root. Make any difference to you, mister, if I stand up for a while."

Oscar was watching Hannah Hudson with a detached interest. "Suit yourself. I can discuss business standing as well as sitting down."

"What business was that?" Hannah said.

Camilla's lips twisted in a mocking grin. "You know perfectly well what he's talking about. Why else do you think you've been kept here all this time? We want your signature on these papers."

"If I do sign them, what guarantee have I that you'll let the three of us go?"

"My dear woman, you have my word on that. Of course, you and the others would have to stay here a little while longer. Until we have a buyer for the hotel. Then you'll be free to go."

Lori edged closer to her aunt. "Don't listen to him, Aunt Hannah. Can't you see he isn't to be trusted?"

"You stay out of this," Camilla said threateningly. "If you know what's good for you."

Lori had to keep talking to distract them from looking at Rex, who was inching closer and closer to the table.

"You aren't the first person they've swindled money from. That's how they make their living. Once you sign those papers, they won't have any further use for you."

Oscar and Camilla were both glowering at Lori. Gone was their interest in Rex Fraser or Aunt Hannah, for that matter. She didn't know what to expect now, only that she had to keep their attention on herself.

"I'd hoped that we wouldn't have to resort to violence to get you to sign those papers, Hannah," Oscar said. "But it seems we have no choice."

Having said those words, Oscar started toward Lori. Rex took that moment to act. He moved quickly and surely. With one swipe of his arm, the lamp crashed to the floor pitching the room into darkness.

Lori reached for Aunt Hannah, who stood rigidly beside her. There was a shuffle and a flash of gunfire and the sound of a struggle going on.

Someone brushed against Lori and she knew it was Camilla. Lori released her hold on Aunt Hannah as she grabbed Camilla's arms. Camilla was strong, but Lori had youth on her side.

She remembered that Camilla had been holding the gun in her right hand. Lori released her hold on Camilla's left arm and, using both hands, groped for the hand holding the deadly weapon.

Camilla struggled and clawed Lori across the face with her free hand, but Lori gave Camilla's wrist a sudden wrenching twist, and she heard the gun fall to the floor. Now Lori moved quickly behind Camilla and forced her arm behind her back. Camilla gave out a cry of pain and her struggles ceased.

Lori was still holding Camilla's arm when a beam of light split the blackness of the kiva. The light danced around the room until it came to rest on Rex Fraser, who was standing over a prostrate Oscar T. Owens. With a quick move, Rex reached down and picked up Oscar's gun.

"Are you all right, Lori?" Rex asked, shielding his eyes against the glare of the flashlight.

"She's fine," came the voice of Aunt Hannah who switched the light from Rex to where Lori stood behind

Camilla. "There's a lot of the Hudson streak in her."

Aunt Hannah moved spryly across the shadowy room and picked up the gun Camilla had dropped. Then she righted the lamp, found some matches, and touched a flame to the wick.

"That's better. Now let's see what damage has been done," Aunt Hannah said with one hand on her hip.

Lori released Camilla, who rushed to her husband's side. By this time Oscar T. Owens was sitting up; there was a dazed expression on his face.

"You're all right, too, Rex Fraser," Aunt Hannah said. "Good thinking to overturn that lamp. And you weren't any slouch when it came to dealing with our shady friend there. What line of work are you in?"

It was then that Lori told her aunt that Rex was a policeman. A detective, he corrected her.

Aunt Hannah took it all in stride, then said, "You got what you came for. Don't you think we ought to be getting these two back to the hotel?"

"My very next suggestion," Rex said as he helped Oscar to his feet.

Oscar and Camilla went along grudgingly and with as much dignity as they could muster. Rex was behind Oscar, with Lori at his side. Aunt Hannah was keeping a close watch on Camilla. The walk through the narrow passageway was not as terrorizing as it had been before. Still, Lori was relieved when they arrived at the surface of the kiva.

Aunt Hannah stared at the entry way for a brief moment before she said, "Can't say I'll be sorry not to see that place again. Got to hand it to those two, though. They sure came up with a good hiding place."

From the shadows there was a sudden noise and Lori turned in the direction of the sound. Someone was hurrying toward them. Aunt Hannah, who still held the flashlight, directed its ray at the approaching figure.

Even in the diffused beam of the flashlight Lori could tell at a glance who the stranger was. Sharon.

CHAPTER TWENTY

"Rex! I got here as soon as I could," Sharon said as she came rushing breathlessly up to where Rex stood. "Of all the times to have a flat tire."

Lori's heart sank as the beautiful brunette drew nearer. Even in the unflattering glare of the flashlight, there was no mistaking her beauty.

"Looks as though I'm too late. You seem to have everything under control."

"It was touch and go for a while down there. But I had some great help. If I'm ever in a tight spot again, I want Lori and Hannah Hudson in my corner."

Aunt Hannah had been appraising the new arrival. "Who is she?" Aunt Hannah asked with characteristic bluntness.

"Hannah Hudson and Lori, I want you to meet my partner. This is Sharon Bisbee. She's been working with me on this case."

Lori stared at the beautiful girl. For a moment it was hard to believe that this delicate, beauteous person could be a detective. Yet, why not? Lori thought. If she had fooled Lori, then she probably would be able to deceive a lot of other people.

"Pleased to meet you," Sharon said, shaking Aunt Hannah's hand. "How are you feeling, Miss Hudson? You

177

don't know how worried Rex and I were about your safety."

"It wasn't so bad. Now that it's all over, anyway. Only, I could sure use a good cup of coffee right about now."

"I'll fix you one when we get back to the hotel," Lori said.

Sharon smiled at Lori. "You must be the niece. Rex has told me a great deal about you."

Lori wondered just what Rex had said, but Sharon was so friendly, it was difficult not to like her.

"Let's get started back to the hotel," Rex said as Sharon handed him some handcuffs, which he clamped on both Oscar and Camilla's wrists.

"Don't want to lose track of you two after all the time I've spent hunting you down."

Lori walked beside Aunt Hannah, who was weaker than she let on. Halfway to the hotel, Aunt Hannah allowed Lori to take her arm, and she leaned against her niece for support.

"Sorry that you had such a bad experience when you arrived here, Lori. Wouldn't blame you in the least if you packed up and hightailed it back to Ohio."

Lori patted her aunt's hand. "You are not going to get rid of me that easily. Whatever happened back there is over and done with.There is still a lot of summer left. Unless you don't want me to stay on."

Aunt Hannah sighed happily. "Lori, you're free to stay as long as you like. Only, I can't guarantee this kind of excitement for the rest of the summer."

They both laughed then and Lori noticed that Rex, who was walking ahead, turned and eyed them curiously.

"You like that fellow, don't you?" Aunt Hannah said after Rex had continued his stride.

"He's nice. It's just that I'll only be here for the summer and—"

"And what? Nobody's pushing you into anything. That is unless you want to be pushed. You could do a lot worse, you know."

Lori very well knew that. She understood a lot of things more clearly now. She knew now why Rex could not tell her about Sharon. He did not want to let his or her identity be known.

In a way Rex had been protecting her. He had watched over her while she had been at the Crying Winds. Still, she couldn't help but wonder whether the relationship between Rex and Sharon was purely business or not.

When they arrived at the hotel, Rex and Sharon took Oscar and Camilla into the living room, while Aunt Hannah sat wearily on the sofa. Lori went to the kitchen and made coffee. As she was fixing a tray, Sharon walked in.

"Anything I can do to help?" she asked in a friendly way.

"I don't think so. I believe I have things pretty much under control."

Sharon smiled. "I know. That's all I have been hearing from Rex is how well you know your way around the kitchen."

Lori studied the brunette's face for a trace of mockery. There was none. "So he has mentioned me."

"Mentioned you. You're all he ever talks about. You and the case. Just between the two of us, he's crazy about you."

Lori wished she could believe the woman. Rex had at one time seemed interested in her, but now she wasn't so certain.

"Surely the two of you must have talked of other things. You are together a lot of the time."

Sharon nodded her head in understanding. "If it will put your mind at ease, I'm married, Lori. Married to a wonderful, understanding man who lives in Denver. I can hardly wait to wrap up this case to get back to him."

Hearing Sharon speak those words was like feeling a great weight lifted from her shoulders. Sharon was married. She was not interested in Rex. What Lori had imagined when she had seen the two of them in the restaurant in Santa Inez was only that, imagination.

"Now, why don't you let me help you with that tray? After all, I've practically had a good night's sleep. That is, I did have until Rex called me and told me what was going on out here."

When they returned to the living room, Isabel Jessop was there. Seeing Lori, she raised her arms in a dramatic gesture.

"Lori, I'm so glad to see you safe and sound. All of this has been going on right under my nose and I wasn't even aware of it. Why it's straight out of a movie I once did for Warner Brothers!"

Lori felt she had returned to the real world again. Aunt Hannah was just as mesmerized as everyone else who met the fading beauty. When Isabel Jessop cast her spell, it was difficult to not fall under its hypnotic influence.

After the coffee had been consumed and Isabel had drained every last drop of drama she could out of the situation, Rex got to his feet.

"I'm afraid we'll have to call it an evening. Sharon and I have to take the Owens couple in to be booked. You will probably have to testify at the trial, Hannah."

"My pleasure," Aunt Hannah said, ignoring the surly stares she received from Oscar and Camilla. "As for right now, I'm going to bed. Sleeping in a chair isn't too bad, but I wouldn't want to make a steady diet of it."

After Aunt Hannah had gone to bed, Isabel Jessop drifted off to her quarters. Lori walked to the door with Rex and Sharon and watched as they herded the Owenses into a waiting car.

As Lori stood in the doorway, Rex hurried across the patio toward her. "Sorry this has to be so abrupt, Lori. I'll be back in the morning. You do understand things a little better, don't you?"

Lori nodded.

"I couldn't tell you who I really was. The less you knew about me, the safer it would have been for you."

Again Lori nodded.

"Take care of your aunt and try to get some rest. I'll see you in the morning."

Before he left, Rex took Lori in his arms and she willingly let him brush his lips against hers. Then he was gone.

Lori bolted the door out of habit and walked around the house, turning the lights out. When she came to Aunt Hannah's room, the door was open a crack. She gently eased the door open further and saw that Hannah Hudson was in her bed and fast asleep.

The wind cried throughout the house as Lori went to her bedroom. Only, this time it was not a mournful or ominous sound. It was almost music to her ears as it lulled her to sleep. A sleep made up of pleasant dreams, of soft lights and good feelings and mostly Rex Fraser.

Lori was awakened by the aroma of bacon and coffee. She dressed quickly and hurried into the kitchen. Aunt Hannah was busily working away at the stove.

"Morning, Lori. Slept like a baby. Never realized how comfortable that bed was until I couldn't sleep in it."

Lori went to her aunt and kissed her on the forehead. It was so natural and Aunt Hannah responded by giving her an affectionate hug.

"You been doing all the cooking around here, Lori?"

"That was the way Camilla wanted it. Frankly, I suspect she wasn't much of a cook."

"In that case I'll leave it to you. I'm going back to my

room and pack those wigs. They give me the willies."

At breakfast the Neeleys were introduced to the real Hannah Hudson and told the story of what had been going on at the hotel. Lori didn't know if it was herself or if the Neeleys had changed, but they appeared very friendly and warm.

While Nancy was having a second cup of coffee, she said, "Lori, I hope you have forgotten what I said to you the other day. I realize how awful I must have sounded. Would you accept my apology?"

"Of course. Let's just forget the whole thing," Lori said, happy that Nancy Neeley was no longer angry at her.

The morning stretched ahead of her and Lori busied herself in cleaning the living room and dining room. At eleven o'clock Rex walked in the front door. Lori ran to greet him.

"Well, that takes care of the Owens caper. They won't be bothering anyone for a long while. At least I hope the jury sees it that way."

"I can't believe what happened. It's all sort of like a fuzzy dream."

Rex smiled at her and his gold-flecked eyes were warm and concerned. "Sorry about what happened to you in the ruins the night you went there alone. I should have been watching more closely."

"That's all right. Will I have to testify at the trial?"

Rex nodded. "But that's a long time off. In the meantime, I hope you can enjoy the rest of the summer."

Lori hadn't thought until now that Rex would be leaving. Now that the Owenses were apprehended, he would have no reason to stay.

"Now that the case is solved, I suppose you'll be getting another assignment."

"It's my job. As I told you before, Lori, I travel a lot in my business."

Dinner that evening was a joyous occasion. Lori had even baked a cake to celebrate the rightful owner's returning to the Crying Winds. She made every effort to appear lighthearted, but the thought of Rex leaving was always in the back of her mind. He wasn't even staying at the hotel anymore.

Two days later Rex came by for his things. Lori couldn't bear to watch him load up his car, and when she heard him come to the door, her heart was in her throat.

"I'll write to you, Lori. If you'll promise to write back."

"You know I will," Lori replied, although it was difficult for her to speak.

Aunt Hannah came into the room at that moment and Lori knew that she couldn't break down and cry in front of her. Together she and Hannah watched as Rex hurried across the patio, pausing at the wrought-iron gate to throw her a kiss.

After he had driven away, Aunt Hannah put a comforting arm around Lori's shoulders. "He'll be back, Lori. If ever there was a lovelight in somebody's eyes, Rex Fraser has it."

For the next two days Lori kept busy. She even helped Aunt Hannah with the rooms to break the monotony of her work schedule. On the third day she drove into Santa Inez to do some personal shopping. She wanted to take back some momentos of New Mexico to give to her parents when she returned to Ohio.

Returning shortly after eleven, she was met by Aunt Hannah, who was waving a letter in her hand.

"It's from Rex. I told you he would write," Aunt Hannah said, sharing the excitement she saw in Lori's face.

The letter was postmarked from somewhere in California. Rex told her he had had to catch up on paperwork. That was why he hadn't written sooner. He told Lori how much he thought about her and tried to sound as light-hearted as possible.

Lori reread the letter at least twenty times that afternoon, and it lay on the nightstand by her bed when she went to sleep that night.

She answered Rex's letter and for the next few weeks they kept the postal service busy with their correspondence.

On a Friday evening, just after dinner, the telephone rang. It was Rex.

"Rex! It's so good to hear your voice," Lori cried.

"You don't know how I've missed hearing yours," he answered. "I've got some great news. I'll be in Santa Inez on Monday. The Owens trial starts then."

Lori could hardly believe her ears. Rex back in New Mexico. Just hearing his voice sent her morale soaring. The next two days dragged endlessly.

When Monday came and she saw Rex, she knew that she was still in love with him. The trial was an ordeal for Lori, but with the testimony of Rex and Hannah Hudson, the jury reached a quick verdict. The judge read the sentence imposed on Oscar and Camilla and Lori couldn't help feeling sorry for them.

"Don't feel sorry for them," Rex said over coffee later at the Crying Winds. "They had a choice and they chose the wrong road."

To cheer Lori up, Rex suggested dinner for two that night in Santa Inez. Aunt Hannah was more than happy to see the two of them going out to dinner.

"It's high time I tried my hand at cooking again. After all, when you go back to Ohio, I'll have to do it all myself."

As it happened, Hannah's old cook ironically turned up before Lori and Rex left for Santa Inez. She had quit her latest job and wanted to return to the Crying Winds.

"Looks as though you may be out of a job," Rex said to Lori as they drove along the twisting road toward Santa Inez.

"I'm glad. For a while I was worried about leaving Aunt Hannah without anyone to help her."

Rex turned to face Lori. "Then you're still planning on returning to Ohio when the summer is over?"

Lori gazed at his handsome face. "Of course. Where else would I go? There is still the matter of college I have to finish."

"Couldn't you complete your education at another school? There are other colleges outside of Ohio. Or so I've been told."

Rex had turned his attention back to the road. Lori continued to stare at his profile.

"Why would I want to do that? There isn't any reason to go to another college."

"I know a very good reason. Only, you'd have to agree to it. And you'd have to wait a little while."

"What are you saying?"

"I'm saying that I'm in love with you, Lori. I'm asking you to marry me. Wherever I'm sent, I want you to be with me. Then, after a year or so, I'll be staying in one place. And you can finish college then. What do you say?"

Lori glanced in the rearview mirror and saw The House of the Crying Winds slowly disappear as the car eased around a curve in the road. It had seemed just like yesterday that she had arrived. But so much had happened since that day in Santa Inez when Rex had met her at the bus depot.

"Well, what do you say?" Rex said, interrupting Lori's thoughts.

"I say—yes. Yes, darling." The words came from her heart.

Rex reached for her hand, which he held tightly, lovingly, all the way to Santa Inez.

Made in the USA
Charleston, SC
13 October 2013